THE MEMOIRS OF ISAAC KENDALL

PAUL ANDRISCIN

BURLINGTON, VERMONT

Onion River Press
89 Church Street
Burlington, VT 05401
info@onionriverpress.com
www.onionriverpress.com

ISBN: 978-1-966607-02-1
Library of Congress Control Number: 2025906201

TO DENISE FOR HER BELIEF IN ME AND SUPPORT AND
FOR ALL THE KENDALL COUSINS.

INTRODUCTION

Old homes that have housed families for generations often give up long kept secrets, and these memoirs are no exception. My wife's maternal ancestral home is in South Woodstock, Vermont, and a few years back, an exciting discovery was made when doing renditions to the basement. A packet of papers was lodged in an old wall in dire need of repair. These were removed by the family and examined. Being a historian, professor, and one of the Site Interpreters at Mount Independence Vermont State Historic Site, they fell into my care. They proved to be a wonderful source of information about one man's experiences during the revolutionary period of the United States.

Transcribing documents is always a challenge, but these were relatively easy once I became familiar with Kendall's handwriting. Isaac Kendall was a well-learned man for his era, probably destined for university had the American Revolution not interfered. His ability to put his thoughts into words makes his diary most interesting, and the biggest reading challenge was that some of the entries were written under less than favorable conditions. I did nothing to change his words or especially, his "voice," merely correcting some spelling and adding necessary punctuations and the footnoting. Kendall's diary runs out in places when he had no paper to continue nor time to write. Here, as he states, he added his recollections years later. These, too, were handwritten but easy to transcribe and seem to have been written with little embellishment when viewed alongside the original diary entries. Although some of the language is perceived today to be politically incorrect, it is accurate for the time period and left unchanged. The only other addition of mine is the separation of Kendall's work into sections to make research easier. Here, then, are *The Memoirs of Isaac Kendall.*

PART I

FROM CONNECTICUT TO THE
NORTHERN FRONTIER

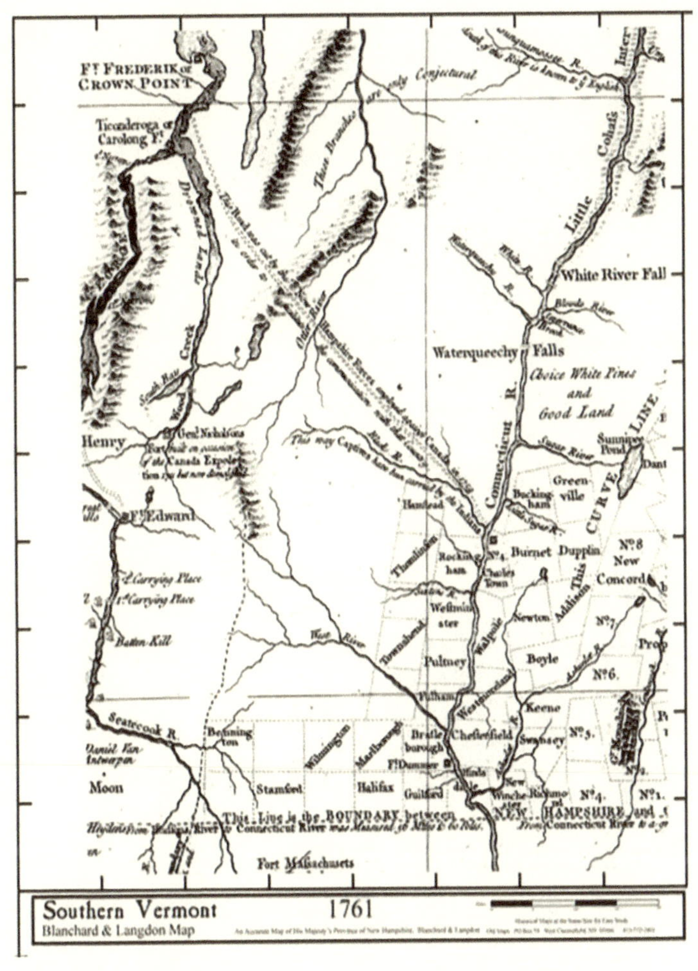

I, Isaac Kendall, do swear that this is the truth as I remember it and that these events are facts as I seen them. Here in my 70th year, I have been accosted by my grand daughter-in-law to put these memories to paper so as to show my grandchildren how we begun this nation and what part I and the rest of the family played in it. Part of this story is my old diary I kept while I was soldiering; some entries I've left out, because they lend little to the story. The rest comes from my recollections, and I've put them in this memoir to fill in the details.

I was born as the only son and second child to Jacob and Esther Smythe Kendall in 1758 in the town of Redding in Fairfield County, Connecticut. I was preceded by one year my sister, Rachael, and was 4 before my sister, Margaret, who we called Peggy, was born. We were church-going Anglicans by preference, as were many of the people living in Fairfield County. We learned to read and write at the church school, as Ma had much stock in education, and saw to it we kept up our studies. I wanted to go to Yale College, but Pa's thinking and the Church and politics made it difficult. You see, much of the state held to the Old Light or New Light Puritan thought, but Redding especially held sway with the Church of England. Many of the neighbors supported King George when the rebellion began, but Pa was different from most and felt the colonies had some real grievances.

My father was a wise man much in tune with the politics of the day. He wasn't a radical; in fact, he used to call the "Sons of Liberty" the "Sons of Lunacy." I was just a child when the Stamp Tax came out. Pa wasn't happy about it but figured we owed a debt to pay for the French war. What upset my father was the Proclamation of 1763 that accompanied it. Without a thought to the colonies, the King set up a proclamation line aimed at protecting his new subjects in Quebec and the lands beyond. This prevented expansion by all the colonies and protected the Indians. King George molly-coddled those red-devils in an attempt to placate them after that warrior Pontiac began his mischief following the defeat of the French who had been their saving grace.

Now, it's been more than 50 years since the Revolution began and many a school child is taught "Taxation without representation is tyranny," but I can tell you those taxes weren't the only issue back in '75. Few in the colonies felt 'twas fair to keep us out of the Ohios. When George III issued his Intolerable Acts following the Tea Party, things got even worse. It wasn't the tax on the tea, believe me.

When the tax on tea was the only one left, it didn't make a lick of sense to protest it so. We rarely had tea on the farm, as 'twas a bit of a luxury, so paying less than a ha'penny for a pound of tea wasn't a problem. Then those hot-heads in Boston destroyed all that tea and cost the Parliament thousands of Pound Sterling as a result. Then came the inevitable follow up, the Coercive Acts, as England called them. Intolerable Acts, they were to us. First, they closed the port of Boston. Hurt them economically. Next, they limited Massachusetts' charter and gave more control to Parliament over the colony. Took away the right to a fair trial by allowing the governor to send anyone he deemed radical to be tried in London. Of course, by then the governor was General Thomas Gage. Few could expect leniency.

More troops came as a result. They were to be quartered in private homes rather than public buildings. "An Englishman's home is his Castle," goes the old saying. If so, how could the King demand we take in his soldiers? The freedom of all citizens throughout all the colonies were put at risk by the acts set down by the King and Parliament. But that wasn't the end of it.

In 1774, King George issued his Quebec Act. This did us all much disfavor. First of all, the Proclamation Line was extended and more troops would come to protect the Indians. Lands that are part of our western states were given to Quebec, Ohio, Indiana, and Illinois among them.

A new governor was to be sent to Quebec to keep that area separate from the other colonies. Their French civil code was allowed and, of all things, Catholics were permitted to vote. Not only vote, but the Catholic Church could tithe money for their church. These may seem trivial matters today, but back in 1774 and '75 they were explosive. Papists voting? Why, it has only been a few years that some states allowed Catholics to vote here in the United States. We members of the Church of England had fought Catholics for control of England back in the days of King Henry and Queen Elizabeth. Of course, some of the tax money levied on the colonies would go to the Church of England, so Catholics and other Protestant denominations had been paying support to that church for decades.

So there it is. Pa had other grievances besides a few taxes. Then came another influence in his life. Pa had read Paine's *Common Sense* and greed with much of the sentiment put forth in its pages. He often quoted, "We have it in our power to begin the world over again," to me and said Paine was "prophetic." In the spring of 1776, he gave me permission to join the militia, so join I did.

Our Connecticut General, Benedict Arnold, a hero and not yet the infamous traitor, was in headlong retreat from Quebec, after assaulting that fortress city the previous December. Some of the locals joined that expedition and never returned. A few other lucky fellows came back with the most incredible stories of traveling through the wilderness of what is now the state of Maine and participating in an attack on Quebec City in a swirling snowstorm on New Year's Eve of 1775. When their enlistments gave out in early January, they struggled back as best they could. But I wasn't there and can't tell anything more of their plight.

Then, in the spring of 1776, the British were reinforced and beginning to move towards Montreal, pushing what was left of Arnold's army in front of them. The call came out for more troops to help save them, and I joined with some other like-minded fellows, and we moved up the old Redding Road to Danbury where we signed on as replacements for Charles Burrall's Connecticut Regiment, which was already sent to Canada that past February.[1] Burrall's men had signed up for a full year, with their term expiring the following January of 1777. In late April, we signed on as nine-month men.

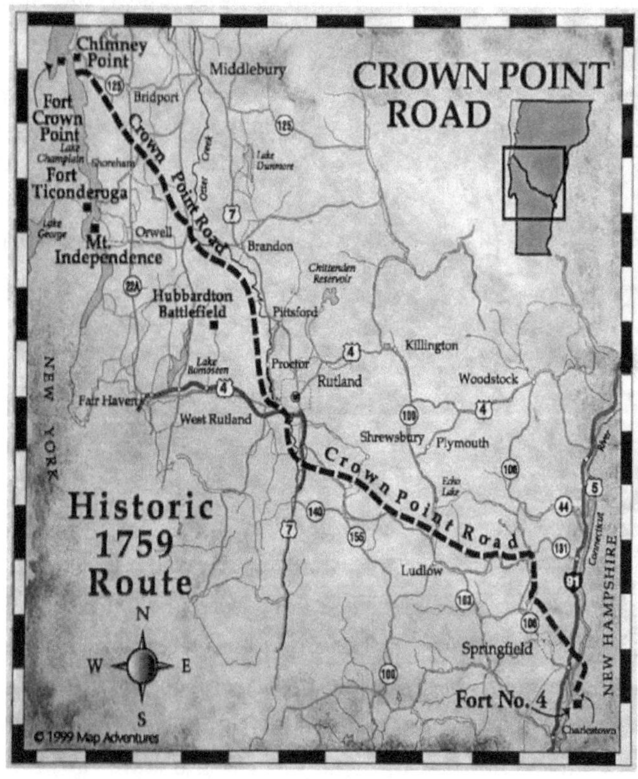

Once we mustered up in Danbury, we headed east towards the Connecticut River and met up with more recruits from the eastern side of the state. More sympathy for the rebel cause existed the farther away you got from Fairfield County and the effects from the Tory-sympathetic New York City on the population. As we neared the south-western border of Massachusetts, we were in with some of the most radical thinkers I have ever encountered. Many wished a complete break with England, which was something I had not yet thought about. Looking back, I still wonder why and how we managed it.

When we got to the Connecticut, we boarded flatboats for the trip up the river. Just guessing, as I never did know our exact number, there had to be 300 to 400 of us. We rode all the way to Fort Number Four in Dummerston, New Hampshire. There we were ferried across the river to the Hampshire Grants, now the state of Vermont, and began to muster into small groups. I was placed in a sizable mix of men destined to join Burrall's Regiment, about 150 of us, under the command of a certain Lt. Trent and two sergeants. These men were veterans, or better said, had been with the unit since its creation back in January 1776. They'd come back from Canada to do recruiting in Connecticut and now were heading north with us. We mustered some muskets and ammunition for those who had none, tents, equipment, cooking gear, and two wagons with mules and five head of cattle. We were to check out the gear, secure ourselves, and move out as soon as we had done so. Within a day or two, we were ready to move, and we headed out over the Crown Point Military Road for points west.[2]

The road been built in 1758 or '59, scantly a year or so after my birth, and not used much since. Made by and for Amherst's moves against the French in that late war, it saw little use until our need for it recently. Fortunately, many had preceded us over this path, and it had become slightly worn. Most of the grown-up briars and brambles were hacked away, but it still had axle-high tree stumps, swampy areas, and no place to turn around if someone was coming the other way with a wagon. Corduroy was laid in many of the wet areas to facilitate the wagons, but there were still some places where 'twas likely we'd get the wagons stuck. Every 15 miles or so, there was a cattle pen built so as to rest stock moving across the mountains. We'd make about that much mileage a day.[3]

Although 'twas April and spring was upon us, those Green Mountains still held deep amounts of snow; cold, frigid nights; and occasional spring snowfalls. The going was slow, and we had hard traveling to make that 15 miles a day. The nights were sometimes below freezing; our blankets were very thin, and we rarely pitched our tents as we tried to make the most of the daylight for traveling. Some of the men were beginning to come down with sickness, probably due to the fatigue and cold. We had no doctor and were miles from any sizable town. We did come upon a tavern stop the second day and made camp there. The officers made use of the tavern's accommodations while we slept in the dooryard.[4]

We spent one memorable night a few days into our journey. We had been moving uphill for the better part of the day before we descended into a nice valley with a slow-moving stream where we camped. Quiet and peaceful without a house or farm nearby, we spent a well-rested night after crossing a series of snow-covered mountains. A creek nearby provided some fresh fish for our supper. The next day, we moved out to the worst part of our journey.[5]

It began to snow almost as we started moving that morning and continued throughout the day. Thick, heavy, wet, clinging snowflakes soaked all of us before we had moved scarcely a mile. The road went nearly straight uphill, switching back here and there to keep the elevation from being too drastic. Did we make five miles that day? I scarcely believe so. We stumbled into a flat area after cresting that mountain and began to set up camp. The snow continued to fall as we worked to gain some comfort for the night. We erected the tents, packed what snow we could around them to keep us warm, and crawled in without suppering. The snow continued and the wind howled around us all night long. We awoke the next morning to bright sunshine and dug ourselves out of about twelve inches of snow. We'd lost two of our number to the cold that night; they were frozen to death with a grim smile on their faces. We buried them best as we could before moving on. 'Twas the first dead men I'd ever seen, but they wouldn't be the last.[6]

The next day brought us out of those mountains and into a valley between the Green Mountains and another range. We crossed Otter Creek a few miles in using a stoutly-built bridge that had weathered the years and followed its opposite shore, swinging to the north. The creek was a little swollen with all the melting snow, which made our path muddy, but we managed with just a little difficulty. Nearby, a freshet provided the sweetest water I've ever tasted. We took a short rest there, filling our canteens and looking across at the mountains we'd just crossed.

We camped on a small rise along the west side of Otter Creek just a few miles down the road, where another small stream entered and the community of Rutland sat in a ways from the opposite shore. Rutland was just a small community in its beginnings and nothing like the big towns and cities we were used to back in Connecticut. Not knowing the populace's politics, since we were now in the Hampshire Grants, we kept to ourselves just outside of town. As it turned out, these folks supported our cause and were more concerned that we were Yorkers sent by their governor to make trouble.[7]

Fishing was good at the mouth of the creek, and the weather had warmed some since we'd left the mountains. We feasted on fresh trout that night and spent a relatively comfortable sleep at our camp. 'Twas the next morning when Lt. Trent brought a local physician, whose name has eluded my memory, and told us we were to be inoculated against the pox. Fear gripped me, as I remember; this was nothing I had bargained for. To be vaccinated for smallpox at this time was to be given the pox itself.[8] We spent about a week recovering from our vaccine, a little uncomfortable at times but well cared for and fed. The symptoms were mild, and within a few days, most of the men were back to soldiering.

We followed the creek again in the morning, passing a small falls about a mile from our campsite. Men were working on the shore opposite the falls, beginning to build what was to become a fort to maintain a military presence in the Hampshire Grants and the town of Rutland.[9]

The Military Road followed a narrow valley with the Otter Creek between the hillsides. These mountains looked different than the Greens we had crossed earlier. They had outcroppings of whitish colored rocks, which shown in the sunlight. After a while, we could hear a crashing sound off to the east; this turned out to be the Great Falls of the Otter Creek descending more than 100 feet.[10] We continued along this way for a while until we reached the Ticonderoga Branch of the Crown Point Road. With Otter Creek long gone and the main road heading north, we moved west towards the Champlain Valley and less mountainous terrain.[11]

This area was nothing but wilderness and forests with no human inhabitants—or none that I could see. The land undulated with hills and vales but no mountains. The mountains we'd crossed some weeks before had ranged from north to south to the east while yet another series of slopes dominated the west. Some abandoned cabins, more like hovels, were dotted here and there. Occasionally, there was a sign that someone had tried their hand at clearing land but nothing to suggest a farm, town, or village. The Military Road split here with the main portion heading to Crown Point. The branch we took led to the old fort called Ticonderoga; it seemed less traveled and more rugged. 'Twas more path than road.

When we arrived at the fort, we found many men already occupying the fort's barracks and surrounding fortifications. These were men from other units newly arriving to the area, mostly from Massachusetts and New Hampshire. The fort itself sits on a point of land in Lake Champlain where La Chute, the water from Lake George, empties. Along the shoreline are the ruins of the old French village. Across the lake on the shore of the Hampshire Grants is a rocky peninsula where yet another creek enters the lake. It is an untamed forest and, at the time, appeared quite useless to us. The fort itself was in rough shape, having been partially destroyed by the French during the last war. The powder magazine and the walls near it had been blown up by the French when they'd abandoned it. The British did little in the way of repairs, as it had become an outpost unnecessary to the defense of the Realm up until now. Some of the other walls had tumbled down due to lack of maintenance, but still 'twas a useful fortification and some work was already being done to render it so again. We all felt assured we could make it into the most formidable bastion it once was with some time and manpower.

It had to be early June by then, and our regiment was still in Quebec. Trent began to prepare us for travel down the lake to join them when word came that they were in retreat and heading towards us. All the empty bateau from there and Lake George were being sent north to evacuate our army. Also came the news of the death of General Thomas to smallpox and of the army's defeat at the Battle of Three Rivers.[12]

We decided we'd wait there for them. On or about the 20th of June, we heard the army had reached St. Jean's and was moving up the lake towards Isle aux Noix to make a stand. The wounded and the sick were to be sent to Crown Point. We were to stay put. The army stayed on Isle aux Noix for nearly a week, and the British did nothing. But following an attack and massacre of some soldiers by British Indians, the army moved south.[13]

While we waited, we worked on fixing the fort. It was a task to relieve the horrid specter of boredom that had entered our ranks. The heat and humidity took some who hastened their deaths by staying exposed in the Sun. Others sought amusement with the bones of Abercrombie's men, which had been lying about for the past 20 years, by making drinking cups from skulls and tent pegs and pins from shin bones; some men even made Ninepins from bones for gaming while others turned finger bones into dice. 'Twas a most morbid sight for decent Christian men to see. As a result, the officers put us to work. We cut timbers to repair the stone barracks, cleared rubble from the blasted magazine, and began to excavate the baker's ovens. Shore batteries were being prepared along the eastern approaches; the Old French lines had been examined and were being attended to. Ticonderoga was beginning to look like a fort again, and we felt we could defend ourselves from there when the time came. And more men began arriving, some from Quebec, others from the lower Colonies, especially from Pennsylvania and the Jerseys.

When our regiment arrived, they were a pathetic shell of a fighting force. Gaunt and emaciated, these men had been through starvation and disease. There were less than 200 of them. With the addition of our numbers, we scarcely reached 350 men available for duty. They were in wont of uniforms and equipment. We had little to give them. We shared what we had, bonded with the veterans, and gained their acceptance. We became a regiment again.

It was probably early July when camp gossip began suggesting we would be moving across the lake to the eastern shore to begin an encampment there. Almost to a man, the idea of leaving the safety and comfort of the fort seemed an absurd idea. What fools could have come up with such a decision? We couldn't believe we would be sent to pursue this notion and some officer would correct the madness of making a fort in the wilderness. But 'twas not to be.

PART II

BUILDING A CITY IN
THE WILDERNESS

Oh, protest our officers did, for they saw the folly in this notion. They were not alone and were joined by officers of other regiments chosen to embark with us in this endeavor. And worse yet, 'twas only New England units being banished across the lake. The regiments from Pennsylvania and New Jersey were to stay on the west side of Champlain. We cried "foul" to no avail. We cited the prejudice of Colonel Wayne, a Pennsylvanian, making a favored gesture for his precious Middle Colony men. We cajoled; we threatened mutiny, whined, begged, whimpered, and schemed, but our cries fell on deaf ears. Ultimately, we moved across the lake and into the wilderness that was East Point, or Rattlesnake Hill.[14]

Ah! The weather that summer was fickle. Heat with its accompanying bugs was joined by thunderstorms and heavy rains. Some men in other units drowned in their tents while sleeping as the water rose quickly due to the removal of all the vegetation by us and the shallow, rocky ground. Rattlesnakes remained a problem and care needed to be taken when moving around in the rocky outcrops. Added to these challenges, food was not yet scarce but not plentiful either. Between the heat, insects, rain, and snakes, this place did not endear itself to us.

'Twas no place for a civilized man to be. Briars and brambles, thickets under giant chestnuts, oaks, maples, and pines teeming with swarms of biting insects searching for a host rounded out the hellish heat generated during the long days. This turned July into a Hades we did not anticipate when we enlisted, nor deserved. Yet, we persevered. We spent the days clearing brush and building a camp. The soil here was shallow with many a rocky outcrop that lent themselves to our constructions. The rest of us cut down trees for them to use, move, dug, and leveled the ground and built foundations for our huts, storage buildings, and officers' quarters.

[Author's Note: Here, as Kendall states, is where his diary begins. At times, he will fill his memoirs with recollections.]

July 23, 1776

Much to explain here. A windfall today in the form of this book; poor fellow from a neighboring hut site had intentions of using it but met a poorly timed demise due to his disagreement with a tree. No one with his group wanted it, so it is mine. As time is plentiful and work becomes finished for the day, it will prove most relaxing to put my thoughts to paper. The trick will be to keep pen and ink or some writing device at hand. This, then, is my first entry.

We dig; the earth is hard and the rocks are unforgiving when the spade cleaves into them. It jars our joints and fatigues our muscles. We fell trees; our axes dull quickly and there is a shortage of sharpening wheels with which to sharpen them. The trees are massive brutes and have been growing here for decades, if not centuries. Maple, chestnut, hickory, and ash. Hardwoods hard as rock. White pine, cedar, and hemlocks only slightly less forgiving. So we work twice as hard to drop the trees. We split huge trunks and turn them into building materials, beams, planking, flooring. Some of the men have carpentry skills; others split shingles. These men set about building our shelters and take pride in their work. No hovels for the men of Burrall's Regiment; we will live in proper housing. Not so for some of the other regiments. Their houses resemble pigsties with poor construction, no windows, fireplaces not properly ventilated so the smoke palled within. These places stink of wood smoke, fetid earth, the sweat of men who couldn't or wouldn't bathe, and the slops and garbage of the inhabitants. Men will be lazy if their officers allow it, but not us.

Our cabin is typical of the rest of the regiment; indeed we all pitched in and helped complete everyone's shelters, including Colonel Burall's and the other officers' quarters. They are of stone foundations laid out so as to strengthen and support split wooden walls made from sawn logs by the regimental sawyers. Assembled with nails and reinforced with cross braces, the walls are stout and sturdy. They have a dirt floor that we try to keep dry, and a fireplace with a stone chimney higher than the roof for good draught effect. The roof is made from split oak or cedar shingles, made by men of the regiment who have carpentry or coopering experience. Each and every hut in Burall's boasts a window made with greased parchment to let in light. The officers' quarters even have sawn plank floors. We have the finest shelters on the hill!

There are eight of us all together in our shelter after we finished it this late July. Myself, Hezekiah "Zeke" Prentiss, Benjamin McCool (who we call Finn), and Harold Moss enlisted together back in April and have been together ever since. I'm sure we are the only ones who had the 'Pox inoculation. Owen Harnish and Lewis Jerome arrived a few weeks after our group with another batch of replacements. Eugene "Flip" Johnson and George Darwin rounded out the group and are veterans who have been with the regiment since January. Their experience is obvious and they see to it we do things right. Flip is a corporal and nominally in charge and takes his nickname from his favorite drink, he tells us. A "Flip" is nearly impossible to attain here at our camp, so

he'll need to await better days to have another. Most days we do have a rum ration of one half gill per man. 'Tis most appreciated by all.[15]

July 24, 1776

Finn McCool and I have earned our wages today. We felled a monster oak the breadth of which was so that with our hands joined together our fingers still could not touch! We began early in the morn with our axes on either side of the tree, and even as the Sun grew high and the day grew hotter, we had made little progress. The axes were wont of honing, and their bite was weak. Finn is a much larger man than I, and his powerful swing consequently did minimal damage to the hard wood of the oak. By the lunch hour, the brute still did not waver. It wasn't until the mid-afternoon that the tree began to give in to gravity. By the time it toppled, we were drenched in sweat and had drawn a crowd! With Finn's accompanying mighty curses, wood chips flying around his head and our oak holding on by a thread of its center, not only our cabinmates and half of our regiment but also men from the surrounding units had come to watch. I, too, had drawn back from Finn's blows and joined the men and officers alike who showed up to see the festivities. The oak fell just before our suppering time with a crash that could be heard across the camp and a tremor that shook the ground beneath our feet. The tree measures nearly five feet across and stood nearly 220 feet high. The highest branches are as thick as a man's thigh. Tomorrow, we will all begin to trim away the leaves, and this tree will become our regimental storehouse. As big as this tree is, we will still need more trees to complete it. As I sit here watching the moon rise, my muscles and bones ache, and I swear even my skin feels weary. Sleep will be a most awaited pleasure, and so I put down my pen and greet Morpheus' awaiting arms.

July 26, 1776

This is our daily routine here so far. Up with the dawn, then breakfast, and a meager one at that. Then we train. Musket drill; load in nine, all of these motions to be done to the beat of a drummer. Half Cock Firelock! Handle Cartridge! Prime your Firelock! Shut your Pan! Charge with Cartridge! Draw your Ramrod! Ram down your Cartridge! Return your Ramrod! Shoulder your Firelocks! Forward March! About Face! Left Face! Right Face! Halt! Poise your Firelock! Cock your Firelock! Take Aim! Fire! But rarely do we fire. And when we march, each order is accompanied by the drum; the changes in the thumping tell us what to do if we can't hear the sergeant's command. We've drilled like this for two days now, and I suspect it shall be our daily task as long as we are here. Some of us find the drill tedious and unnecessary while others see it as a challenge. We are not backwoodsmen reminiscent of the old French Coure de Bois who made their living as trappers and explorers but rather farmers, merchants, clerks, and the like. Sure, I handled my family's old fowling piece to hunt ducks, turkeys, and rabbits, but I never thought I'd be marching and loading like this!

Of course, there is the occasional bayonet drill without bayonets as few of our men have them. Those who don't tie sticks to their muskets. I must admit, this is more of a challenge than the musket drill. I've yet to meet a duck or even a rabbit who gave me cause to wave my fowling piece at them menacingly. However, it has become part of our repertoire. Some of the officers served in the old French wars, and they have taught our sergeants the old drill they learned from the British. We all suspect our sergeant didn't need to be taught the drill. Sergeant Liam O'Toole is our taskmaster; some say he's an Irish Papist, others claim he's a Scot, and there's more than a few who suggest he's a deserter from the old British army during the French War. Either way, he's a drillmaster, and Flip and the other corporals stand by his side and make sure we do our maneuvers. O'Toole stands for no guff and no slacking. He has a piercing stare that'll freeze a man at 50 paces. Combined with fiery red hair and beard, his eyes command your attention when he barks his orders.

So now, we learn to thrust and parry, attack and repel. And then more marching, marching, marching. Lunchtime. Repeat until suppertime. A little target practice now and then, but not much as our powder and ball supplies are not plentiful. Not so with flints as there is a large cropping of flint right here on the hill. Knappers are continually chipping flints for us to use, and there's a knapping shed not far from our camp. The Indians have been using the stone from this place for years, I suspect, as we find arrowheads to be ours for the picking up. We have quite a collection in our cabin already.

July 27, 1776

News came to us today of a momentous decision to break completely away from Britain. The Continental Congress in Philadelphia has declared our independence. Colonel Arthur St. Clair has ordered that the paper, "Declaration of Independence," is to be read to all the troops, and a rum ration doled out to accompany it. Rattlesnake Hill will forever be known as Mount Independence! "God Bless the Free and Independent United States of America" and three "Huzzahs!" were sounded at the end of the reading.

Independence! The word itself has a giddy feel to it. But what does it mean to us at this time? "All men are created equal." Those words stood out when General Gates read them. "Governments instituted men and ruled with their consent." What would the tyrant King George think about that? What would Pa say if he heard this Declaration? Has he? How much of this sentiment can we direct towards Thomas Paine's writing? Pa would have to be pleased; I wish I was somewhere where I could talk to him about it.

We are a new nation. But how can this be? Would the British allow this? What of Congress? What about the men who approved it? Some we knew of the Bostonians' Adams's, and Hancock, Connecticut's Williams, Sherman, and Wolcot, the Virginian Jefferson, and of course, all knew the famous Dr. Franklin. What will become of them? How can this new nation of 13 colonies stand up to the mighty British Army? How can we be an independent nation when the Royal Navy rules the seas and can blockade every port we have? What can we men as soldiers do to save this independence? It seems that now we must be ever ready to defend it![16]

We spent the evening discussing what had transpired as we enjoyed our rum. Some seemed apprehensive about leaving England while others relished the idea. Then the conversation turned to Dr. Franklin, who Flip says was here just a few weeks before our group arrived from Connecticut. Claims he saw the great man at Ticonderoga on his way back from a trip to Montreal where he was trying to gain support for our rebellion and that he was accompanied by a Papist from Maryland. Seems a most odd combination to me, but I sure would have enjoyed a glimpse of the man who conquered lightning![17]

July 30, 1776

As August nears and July is on the wane, our regiment has a camp complete with a headquarters, a storehouse, a small drilling ground, and huts for our shelter. We, as did many other units, started to receiving replacements, and we began turning our constructions to defensive works along the lake shore. Now that we've cleared this peninsula and have moved to building the shore batteries, we can see the wisdom in choosing the position. The actual terrain slides gently uphill to a high spot about a quarter mile from the shore. Here a large battery wall is being built, which will protect the fort from attacks from the north. We are working on fortifying the northern shore to sustain this position, which will include more cannon batteries. Support will come on the west shore from a redoubt being constructed near the edge of the lake closest to our side.[18]

August 2, 1776

Tragedy struck our regiment and especially our cabin today. During one of our musket practices, we lost Owen Harnish. Following his last shot, he lowered his piece and rested his hands on the barrel, placed his chin on his hands, and cleft his skull in twain. His firelock must not have discharged when he thought it had, and the charge went off when he least expected. We laid him to rest in the regimental burial ground, and the reverend said a few words over him. A mere wooden cross with his name marks his grave that cannot possibly endure the ravages of time, so in future days no one will know they are treading across the bones of our friend and fellow soldier. Owen was a quiet man, with two young children back in Connecticut. He will be missed by more than just us in the regiment.

Accidents such as Owen's occur all across the camp and in every regiment. This entire camp has lost more men to accidents and illness than to the enemy and has become a most dangerous place to live and work. Sickness, accidents, poor food, and the ever-present possibility of attack by Savages if you venture beyond the fort's bounds make every day one survives this Hector's Den another day to be thankful for. For these reasons, I fear Owen's death shall not be the last we suffer.

August 4, 1776

Word has come that the British are preparing to move against us. Right now they are in Canada stockpiling men and materials and building ships. Our shore defenses are shaping up rapidly. Artillery pieces arrive almost daily, and men are training as artillerists. Of course, accidents accompany the training. Just this evening, a stunning explosion sent one man into the lake in pieces. Others have been harmed with less deadly injuries from the back-breaking work of just moving the guns into place. Broken bones, cuts, hernias, as well as crushed fingers and toes afflict these men. Slings and bandages have become badges of honor for their heroism.

We've had two other spectacular explosions here the first days of August. Two days ago, as the Sun was setting, a mortar that was being test-fired from a gundalow near the Mount's point blew up, sending half of its body and the shell 20 feet in the air. The sound of the blast caught our attention and we saw the pieces fly. The very next day, another mortar blew up almost the same way. Unbelievably, no one was hurt in either case, but we are now left without any serviceable mortars for our defenses. Three explosions in three nights make me glad I'm not an artillerist.

August 7, 1776

Men and material are constantly arriving here as we move into August. And shipbuilders, too! General Arnold has taken it upon himself to oversee the building of a fleet south up the lake at East Bay near the town of Skenesboro. He has appropriated the saw mill of the notorious Tory and landowner Phillip Skene, who, rumor has it, is in Canada serving the British. These shipbuilders are from Massachusetts and New Hampshire, having been sent here by Congress. Arnold is also enlisting volunteers to help with the construction. I find myself torn between going to help with the boats or staying here and working on our defenses. Both seem equally important to our well-being and safety.

August 11, 1776

Four of us have just returned from four days of working on Arnold's fleet as part of a contingent from the Mount. We are all exhausted from the hardness of the work and the return journey down the lake in the steaming late afternoon Sun. I, along with Flip, Finn, and Zeke, spent the hours laboring, sawing boards, cutting pegs, splitting planks, and caulking seams with pitch. My hands are blistered and rawboned, having not been accustomed to the difference in handling the ship-working tools compared to our usual picks and shovels. The others are suffering the same symptoms as I. I doubt rest will be in store for us on the morrow, but an early turn-in is guaranteed tonight!

August 12, 1776

A good night of sleep and a light duty day will give me time to tell about General Arnold and his fleet. Arnold, as usual, is embroiled in controversy in his new command. He has been fighting with General Hazen over goods taken from Montreal and is mire in a court martial.[19] Meanwhile, he oversees the building of this fleet to gain control of the lake. He has been at this since June and has completed at least three row galleys, with two more near completion and five more with their keels laid.

He runs the shipyard like a man possessed, one minute calling for this, the next for that: "Where is so-and-so? How much of this do we have? When can you finish this? Not good enough! Sooner! I need more men! Damn your eyes! If you're not more careful, I'll have you in irons!" But he seemed most glad to see us and asked especially if there were any Connecticut men amongst our group. When we "Huzzad," he called us forward and gave us a special task. There were about 12 of us assigned to re-assemble the cutter, "Lee," which was begun in St. Jeans back in May and disassembled and then hauled south during our army's retreat in June. Arnold had personally numbered all the boards, and now 'twas our task to put the vessel back together. 'Twas a nightmare! But we persevered and by the time we left, 'twas ready for rigging and final preparations. As tired as I still feel, there is a certain pride knowing I helped build this vessel and this fleet that may indeed save us in the near future.[20]

August 14, 1776

The rumor mill is hard at work as news has come to us that General William Howe has occupied New York City and will soon send 4,000 troops north to occupy Ticonderoga and Mount Independence. We weren't panicked but picked up the pace of our work on the defenses out on the point. Our engineer,

Colonel Baldwin, laid out a new redoubt at the highest spot on the Mount. Men from all the regiments worked to finish it as quickly as possible. Shaped like a horseshoe, this position commands the lake from a northern approach and supports the shore batteries where our heavy guns are.[21]

August 15, 1776

More news comes to us, this time from Canada. Seems one of Whitcomb's men shot and killed a British general in an ambush. A warning was sent to us by none other than General Carleton, which states, "Rebels and traitors! Taking up arms against the King is treason! Flags of truce shall be ignored and persons shall be immediately seized except when they come to implore the King's mercy." The King's mercy, indeed![22] The warning stinks of British treachery; I doubt any of us would receive much less than a visit to one of the rotting prison hulks we have heard about or an execution for treason.

August 19, 1776

It seems our British adversaries are not to be outdone by Arnold's attempt to build a fleet to control the lake. Word comes from Whitcomb's scouts that shipbuilding is being done at the northern end of the lake by the British. Distressing news from our fleet followed closely, describing the command struggle that occurred between Arnold and the Dutchman Wynkoop. We know little of the details, but the end result was the arrest of Wynkoop by Arnold. It seems Arnold is always squabbling with some other officer. A brilliant but prideful man, he seems always to be in some sort of conflict over some trivial issue, many of which could be remedied through calm negotiations. But not our Arnold. Speaking not only for myself, we would follow him anywhere because we know he will not waste us and will be beside us all the time. Still, as a fellow Nutmegger, Arnold's actions are sometimes disturbing.[23]

August 20, 1776

The work here never seems to end. Laboratories, wharves, storehouses, and dozens of other buildings are continually being built on both sides of the lake. We have now more than 12,000 people here, men, women, and children. We have built a city in the wilderness. What seemed to us a stupid idea back in early July is now a most formidable position, even stronger than the old Fort Ticonderoga. Most of the troops are on the Mount side and are from New England. Regiments are here from Connecticut, Massachusetts, New Hampshire, and the Grants, all of whom seem to have no ties to any of the other colonies and desire autonomous command.

Of course, the men stationed at Ti have it much easier than us. They are from Pennsylvania and New Jersey and are of low moral standing. Understandably, they have a low regard for us as well and call us "Dirty Low Yankees"; we call them "Cowardly Rascal Buckskins" and sometimes, I swear, we'd rather fight each other than the British! They are just different than us. Some of them are old English and Scottish stock, but there are Welsh, Germans, Dutchmen, Huguenots, and even some Irish amongst them. Many Negroes are in their regiments, mostly used as laborers to dig and build, and most likely slaves either serving with their masters or sent to serve in their stead. Although we have some Africans in our New England regiments as well, no slave owner from any of our colonies would ever be so callous as to send another into harm's way, slave or freeman. And they have brought women with them. No decent New England woman would ever be seen at an army camp, so these must be of the lowest caliber and station.

But still, there is such a wide gap between all of us here. Massachusetts men despise those from Rhode Island and barely tolerate New Hampshire-elites and us Connecticut men. The rest of us reciprocate anyone from a colony other than our own in kind. But, by far, the most ornery, uncouth, and unrefined of all the troops here are the ones from the Hampshire Grants, who are fiercely independent and loyal only to their commander. They would rather fight New Yorkers than anyone else and indeed had been nearly at war with the Yorkers before this revolution got started. It was these men under Ethan Allen who took Ticonderoga back in 1775, shoving our Arnold into a subordinate role, even though Congress gave him the command.[24] Squabbling, pettiness, lack of toleration, and outright hatred all contributed to our military force defending the newly created nation. I don't know how we will ever accomplish anything.

August 22, 1776

More news comes from Canada: Carleton has sent prisoners on a ship bound for New York or somewhere where the men will rot away on prison hulks in the harbor. This sad news comes on the beginning of three days of heavy rain, which saturated not only everything we possessed but our morale as well. It has rained throughout most of the summer. Our camps are full of puddles held there by the thick, clay soil. The men have troubles just walking through the wet grounds as the clay becomes thick and sticky, clinging to the leather soles of our shoes and making it seem as though we are walking on ice. These puddles become stagnant when the Sun is out and are full of mosquito worms, and there is nothing we can do to drain them. We get swarms of mosquitos every day and night, and they make even the easiest of tasks difficult. We try to fend them off with smoke sticks but to little avail. They so weaken us with their constant harassment that we spend more time fighting the mosquitos than anything else. On top of it all, yellow fever has developed in camp, and men from every unit have been stricken with it. Showing no respect for rank or social betters, the disease has even claimed the life of Lt. Col. Bond of Gardner's Massachusetts Regiment, one of our fellow brigade unit commanders. He was buried with a cannon salute.[25]

August 23, 1776

Once again, tragedy has hit our cabin home; both George Darwin and Harold Moss died of yellow fever. Moss was sent to the hospital with the fever and never returned. George died in our hut last night after shaking, sweating, and delirium. The fever took all he had before mercifully ending his life, and he died a death no one deserves. We buried him in the regimental cemetery with Owen and the others. Within a month, we've lost three men in our shelter. The other huts in our regiment have had similar losses. The rest of us were lucky to not get the disease. Smallpox, the dreaded pox, visits this place frequently, and orders have been issued to forbid inoculations for fear of spreading the disease even more. (The Dunderheads!) Infected soldiers are made to swear an oath that they have not been inoculated, which was drawn up by none other than General Gates himself! I am thankful for Lt. Trent's foresight in having us done last spring. Despite our losses, and even though men are arriving daily here, Burrall's has had no further replacements.

August 24, 1777

It rains heavily today, and we have been excused from all but the most mundane duties. There is a pall over our hut with the loss of our friends and campmates. I can't help but contemplate just how bad our medical care is here. More men seem to go to our hospitals that never come back than those who are cured and released. Of course, there are so many maladies here that can lay a poor soldier low, it's a wonder any of us have survived this long.

Smallpox, yellow fever, typhoid, malaria, diarrhea, dysentery, scurvy, putrid fever, the ague, measles, mumps, tussis, the itch, lice, bedbugs, rattlesnakes, lack of rations, moldy flour, rotten salt pork, supplies coming all the way from Albany and not enough of them, bad water from the lake, men drowning in their sleep because of the heavy rain all lay us low here. At any given moment, half the garrison is sick. Men are dying every day. We bury them as best we can with little ceremony. We have doctors, but they know little. We have a regimental hospital, but it seems a death sentence to be sent there. These are dingy, dark, and smoky places because doctors believe the smoke will clean the putrid air. A few times a week they burn sulfur or tar, sometimes gunpowder when there's enough, to purify the air of the vapors. Fresh straw on dirt floors soon becomes fetid with dysentery victims' slop and remains there until the victim dies or recovers, and only then it is removed and burned.

Treatments are sometimes worse than the disease. They use bloodletting for everything. Open a vein and bleed the man. If an infection appears, the doctors will apply a cataplysm [Author's note: a Cataplysm is a poultice made from wheat bran or flax seed applied to the skin and covered with flannel to relieve pain, swelling or draw out pus] or a formentation to the area to ease the pain and draw out the pus. Without a doubt, however, the most dreaded cure is the clyster, which gives the unfortunate invalid the medication rectally. Then, there are the other purgatives and diuretics given to induce vomiting or bowel movements. For extreme pain, an Anodyne is available if there are sufficient supplies.[26]

We have one surgeon and 45 surgeon's mates for our brigade of what's supposed to be 1,000 men. They are too busy to get every man properly cared for. But they try hard, and some attempt new things. A few doctors began giving tree bark to patients suffering from malaria or the ague.[27] They know fresh fruit and greens will cure scurvy, but there is little of either to be had. A new doctor from another brigade has convinced our surgeon to separate cases and open the rooms to fresh air. Time will tell if this is proper. It is much more frightening to be a potential patient when you realize there is much more about medicine that the doctors need to learn than they already know. Medical science indeed! Better to be called medical guessing, I say!

August 25, 1777

The rains continue, so again a good day to write. The summer has been so wet as to make life uncomfortable for all of us here. Our clothing is soaked through most every day, and there is little we can do about it because, you see, we wear the same clothing day after day as there are no uniforms to spare. We have no coats, breeches, stockings, or smallclothes, and precious little time to wash them or ourselves. Tears and rips in our coats are patched as best we can, and we are continually taking on a more and more ragged appearance. There seems to be little chance of getting replacement clothing. My breeches patches have patches! I'm missing buttons from my jacket; my smallclothes are torn, and my stockings have been darned beyond their serviceability. We scavenge what we can from the dead, as they no longer have need of them, but what we get is not much better than what we already have.

Even our camps are becoming less and less livable. Our sinks are fouled, and men void urine wherever they please. The regimental latrines for all to use are some distance away and send everything over the cliffs to the lake. For some, it's too far to go, and, indeed, some can't wait or make it that far before soiling themselves. Wood parties need to go farther afield to bring sufficient wood back for construction and fire, and the draught animals wear out quickly due to poor fodder and lack of good grazing.

Our diet leaves much to be desired and doesn't come up to what rations are to be. According to our Congress, we are to have one pound and a quarter of beef or pork per day per man. This is to be supplemented by a gill of dried beans or peas, a flour ration, salt, pepper, and vinegar. This is an ideal our commissary cannot live up to.

We have a herd of cattle that provides fresh beef for us. Markers are given to us by our officers, which we give to one of our cabinmates who takes these chits to the quartermaster, who then doles out the meat ration accordingly.

So when there was the eight of us who made up our mess, we should have received a ten pound piece of beef to cook as we saw fit for that day. However, 'twasn't always so, and oftentimes we drew short meat rations. Sometimes we get a good section of beef and can do well with it; other times it is fat and bones, and soup is all it's good for. Orders have been issued by General Gates forbidding us to fry or grill our meats, but it is largely ignored when the beef ration allows for it. We have a grill made of barrel hoops and wire on which we fry steaks over our fires. We've also learned to weave grills out of green sticks, which won't burn rapidly; if we can cut branches from sweet sassafras or birch, our meat takes on some of the flavor from the sap oozing from the twigs.

We also have a large camp kettle, which produces wonderful stews and soups when we have or make the time to cook them. We all take our turn at the meal-making, but Zeke Prentiss is our prize cook. He can take the worst portions of beef, add some of our other rations, and end up with a tasty dish we all can share. A most memorable dish was prepared by Zeke the other night when he took a piece of beef shank and turned it into a thick stew using some flour, watercress we had gathered from East Creek, and some fresh turnips that had been doled out by the quartermaster. By adding some of our vinegar ration, our cabin crew enjoyed a delightful stew.

It is a special treat when we do get dried beans, peas, or lentils; they are eaten with gusto and don't last long. Flour rations don't keep in the wet, damp climate such as we've had this past summer and turn moldy quickly or become bug-ridden, but we do the best we can and devour our breadstuffs, bugs and all.

When we have fresh flour, a quick mix with water and a flat rock in the fire will produce a firecake that is usually burned on the side nearest the fire and uncooked on the other side. Although not quite a gastronomic delight, it is sufficient. We have few utensils but do have our iron kettle and fork and spoon for cooking. Otherwise, we make what we need to get by. I've seen some men use their bayonets as a grilling device. We've taken an old iron bar that we found and bent it into a hook for handling large pieces of beef when we have to move them or hang them around the fire. Along with rocks, we have procured two pieces of bar shot "borrowed" from the artillery to help contain our fire. And of course, our barrel hoop grill fits atop the bar shot to help our efforts.

Sometimes, we get salt pork shipped in barrels from the depot in Albany. Oftentimes, it is rancid despite it being salted; this is due to unscrupulous teamsters lightening their loads by draining the brine, thus exposing the pork to the heat without its salty protection. It is green, streaked with black, and must be soaked in water for some time before we dare eat it. Frying it releases the grease, to which we add flour to make a thick gruel. If we have dried peas, beans, or lentils to soak with the salt pork, we can make a fairly palatable supper.

Occasionally, we fish, although we are discouraged from doing so due to the danger of capture or death. As well, the waters are mighty filthy with the men using the cliffs and lake as a latrine. Mutton, rarely, and poultry, equally rarely, make up the rest of our diet. Wild game has long been either hunted out or driven away, but having venison is not completely uncommon if one of the wood parties gets lucky.

For drink, there is no want of wine; we also have ciders and spruce beer along with the occasional rum ration. The water here is most foul and unpotable. Of course, there is no fresh milk to be had. As August wanes and September draws nearer, I wonder what lies in store for us as winter weather will make it even harder to get supplies, for there is already a feel of autumn in the air.

August 28, 1776

Much of Arnold's fleet has moved up the lake to be fitted with masts, rigging, and artillery pieces. I watched as it moved along and especially felt a point of pride when I spotted the "Lee." She looked as strong a warship as any as she floated by.

A new sawmill is being built, and men have been detached from different units to procure wood to be sawn there. There is a place out near the point and shore batteries that overhangs the lake. It is here we mast the boats by sliding the timbers into place in the hulls. It's hard work, requiring many men and a fair amount of muscle power. The fear of injuring myself always lingers whenever I've been detailed to help mast a boat. Fortunately, I've been lucky and have only been on that detail twice. However, some men are made for that task, men like Finn McCool, who revels in that sort of work. Finn is a giant compared to many. A full head taller than I and of large girth and posture, Finn seems impervious to any sort of physical activities. It is good to have him as a friend, for I am sure I wouldn't want him as a foe.

PART III

DEFENDING THE MOUNT

September 7, 1776

During the first week of September, four of the ships and six gundalows were sent down the lake on a reconnaissance mission. Four scouting parties have also been sent north to find out what the British are up to. Once again, we received heavy rain that washed out all building activities on the Mount. News from New York arrived again. Washington has been defeated soundly and driven from Long Island. The forts along the Hudson have been taken, and thousands of our men have been killed or captured. Generals Sullivan and Sterling have been reported missing.[28] General Washington's army has been dealt a heavy blow and is in complete retreat. It is believed we will lose New York City to the enemy. That would prove to be a most unfortunate turn, as there are more Tories in that city then there are Rebels. If it truly does fall, we may never gain its return. Bad news comes to us almost daily from the south. It is indeed a dark moment for our new nation.

September 8, 1776

Almost the entire camp spent the day working on the shore batteries and artillery positions. An attack is imminent, as Redcoats and Indians have been spotted just north of the forts. With Washington's army in disarray and our own plight uncertain, it has been a nerve-wracking day to say the least. What will tomorrow bring?

September 10, 1776

More of the same work yesterday. Turned in early with the knowledge that today would be more of the same. However, we had more row galleys arrive from Skenesboro, and we spent the day fitting and rigging them for battle. We also heard more bad news from the south, as Washington's army is still fleeing before the British advances. How long will it be before we are attacked?

September 13, 1776

Fitted out yet more galleys yesterday. Loud firing from the north of us told us our fleet was doing something. Today, we found out the fleet had made contact with Redcoats and Canadians near Windmill Point. Not much resulted. Still, we wait what seems to be an obvious attack upon this installation.

September 14, 1776

Cannon fire is regularly heard coming from up the lake. We had no way of knowing if the fleet is engaged. A small force of Canadians and Redcoats has been spotted between here and our position at Crown Point. Things are heating up. The last of the row galleys have arrived from Skenesboro to be fitted and readied for battle.

Word comes to us of a skirmish that occurred between British Regulars, Canadians, and their Indian allies at Windmill Point, which resulted in three of our men dying and some captured Britishers. One of the prisoners turned out to be Thomas Day, an American who had been captured by the British and forced to serve in their army or be executed. He brought information for Arnold as to British shipbuilding activities in which he told of schooners brought to St Jean's. These ships are being deconstructed at Montreal, hauled overland to St. Jean's, and then reconstructed there to create a fleet superior in numbers and firepower that Arnold's. This was not the news we wanted to hear.[29]

September 18, 1776.

Arnold now begins to call for volunteer seamen and supplies. His needs range from pitch to clothing, rope, ammunition and grenades, chains, tar, nails, pulleys, block and tackle, and rum; in short, everything! He and General Gates quarrel over Gate's order to forage on the Grant's side for foodstuffs. To search for anything north of here is to invite attack from British-led Savages. Fifteen of our men have been captured the last few days because of this order. To the south there is nothing but a continually extending wasteland of stumps due to our camp wood parties having to venture farther and farther afield. Supplies from the south have also become difficult to come by, probably because of the weather, which has turned cold, rainy, and miserable. This lack of foodstuffs has resulted in Gates' order, and we wonder what will become of us if we venture in that direction. Arnold's concern for us as always colors his judgment, but as always, he has to clash with someone, and Gates seems to bring out the worst in him.

September 20, 1776

September quickly came on with cold winds and gales and heavy morning fogs that enveloped the lake, and the men came down with fevers and agues. The weather is turning colder rapidly, and we are unprepared. Snow began to cover the Green Mountains to the east by mid-month. Arnold's spies returned from their scout and reported the British fleet would be ready within a fortnight, bringing 7,000 troops with them. More enemy soldiers are being spotted near our forts. The shores have become dangerous for us, and many men have been captured or scalped by the British Indians. Skirmishes between us and the British have increased, sometimes involving the gunboats. I was told that one of our schooners had been shot up during a firefight started by a fake deserter. He lured the boat near the shore where 'twas ambushed by 400 of the enemy lying in wait. After some furious action, it returned with a number of wounded.

September 25, 1776

Finn and I walked the camp earlier this afternoon as we had only light duty this day. As we walked towards the Star Fort, the lay of the land opened up before me, and it was as though I was seeing this place for the first time. The peninsula itself is a bastion of strength sticking out like a thumb into the water. The lake twists around it in the shape of a bent horseshoe. East

Creek flows into the lake on the Hampshire Grants' side, and along the shore of that creek lies thick, impenetrable swamps full of gooey, sticky muck and mud and swarming mosquitoes and other biting insects, along with high cattail reeds. It has also provided us with watercress, inklebaum, and cattail roots to supplement out food stuffs. It is a perfect protective flank for our defenses. Across the lake is the entry point of La Chute River, which flows out of Lake George, another of our supply routes. We can take Lake George to Fort Anne by using Half-Way Creek. Of course, Lake Champlain also extends to Fort Anne by way of Wood Creek, so we have an extensive waterway to use. Our supplies travel from our main supply base at Albany to Fort Edward by Hudson's River, then along a portage to Fort Anne, followed by another trip on the water, so it is crucial to keep the water routes open.

I can hardly describe what has been built here in the past few months and am amazed at the numbers of soldiers here. And not only soldiers, but women and children as well. There are two brigades here other than our own and another over at Fort Ticonderoga as well. General Arnold commands our brigade, and we have the 24th and 25th Continental Regiments along with Porter's Massachusetts Militia to complete our muster. Generals Bond and Stark command the other two brigades here while "Mad Anthony" Wayne leads his Pennsylvanians and Jerseys across the lake.

Every brigade has its own cabins and storehouses. Each has an officers' headquarters and a quartermaster's commissary building. We have our camps set so they all are arranged in the same fashion. This is so we can find the important buildings in whichever brigade we may be.

The old fort has been repaired to render it useful again with a bridge boom to connect with the Mount. A sizable shore battery adds to our defenses against an attack by ship. The old French Lines have been repaired and made formidable again with a forward observation post at Mount Hope to alert us to any enemy activity should it come.

Here, we have constructed shore batteries, another large position on the height above the shore to protect the former if it comes under attack. There are warehouses, smithies, and wrights of all kinds from black to wain, carpenters' shops, saw and grist mills, and gardens and pastures for our horses and cattle. Our First Brigade occupies the highest point of land. In the center is a grand parade ground, and all around it are dozens and dozens of huts, cabins, warehouses, and buildings for our brigade offices of command. We truly have built a city in the wilderness, and I have been told we have more people here than in the city of Boston, a statement I find truly hard to comprehend. It has been proclaimed that we are the third largest city in America? Beyond comprehension!

September 26, 1776

It has been raining all day. The camp is a quagmire of mud. My spirits are low, and my body aches. My knees and feet feel as if they will explode, and I'm hot and cold over and over again. My throat rasps with every spoken word, and I have no desire to eat. Perhaps a good sleep will ward off my illness.

September 28, 1776

Heavy rains continue, and I fear I am ill with tussis, fever, or the ague. I refuse to allow Flip or Finn to take me to the surgeon. I am beat down and can keep little nourishment in my belly.

October 2, 1776

Feeling a little better and having survived my malady, I am ready to resume my duties. Finn found an Indian, one of the Oneidas serving with a Yorker unit, who told him of a poultice of herb for my chest and who gave him a potion of black liquid to cure my fever. Finn told me I was in delirium and they all feared for my life, but the potion brought me around, and the poultice cured my foul stomach and opened my lungs. I owe my life to my hutmates and their concern for me, along with an Oneida I've never met. The Indians are a mysterious people, but sometimes wondrous is the way of the Savages!

October 3, 1776

Feeling better and stronger every day. September ended with a series of nasty storms; October began no better with a solid day of heavy rain on the Third. The few days of rather calm before that, when I was sick, Arnold took the opportunity to move the fleet to Valcour Bay. As soon after the rain as possible, we believe the British will move on us; I wonder how well prepared we are.

October 4, 1776

My cabinmates and I have been ordered to work on a new fortification upon the highest point on this peninsula, which happens to be at the spot of our very own parade ground. I am exhausted this evening after being weakened by my sickness and this work. Every brigade upon our Mount has provided workmen for this detail, and what a job it is proving to be.

Colonel Baldwin has drawn out plans for a new fortress. Hundreds of us worked today digging a continual trench some two to three feet deep wherever the rock allowed us to do so. Other men were cutting down trees to be made into pickets and dropped into the trench. Of course, we are lacking enough tools to do a proper job, so some of us are using pointed branches to break up the soil. Luckily, all the recent rains have rendered the soil soft and easy to dig. Still, it is a massive job that will keep us busy for a while.

October 5, 1776

Another day at work on our picket fort. General Gates has ordered every man to turn out and finish the works. It is beginning to take on a shape and design, and, fortunately for us, our hut is outside the walls and will not be disturbed. It appears to be an eight-sided affair with a powder magazine dug into the ground on the west side. Our parade ground is torn to pieces and has ceased to exist, and, with hundreds of men working, the walls have gone up quickly. It should be finished within a few more days.

October 7, 1776

Our fort is finished; at least the outside walls are done. It is eight-sided in the shape of a star with a large gate facing towards our shore batteries. As I stated before, our regimental parade ground has been gobbled up by the construction, but there is now another to replace it within the fort's walls. Yesterday as we were completing our work, carpenters began their work on the barracks that are to be constructed inside. These barracks and some general office buildings will complete our Star Fort, as the men are calling it. Although it shall take some time until it is done, it is a most formidable bastion, and it dominates the entire Mount. Rumors abound as to an eminent attack upon us. Arnold's fleet is still up north, and no word has come to us as to his activities. 'Tis the plight of every soldier to play the awaiting game.

October 8, 1776

We can do nothing but wait, anticipate, and sit out another rainy, miserable day. I sit here listening to the rain, alone with my thoughts. Finn lies sleeping and snoring in his bunk. Lewis and Zeke are on picket, and Flip has gone on his inspection rounds. I can't help but wonder what is going to happen to us when the British come. Can we hold our works? If we are placed under siege, will Congress see fit to rescue us? Could we breakout if besieged? Where could we go if we left here? Dare we fall back and surrender the lake to the enemy? Would Washington's army shift north to join with us and create a mighty force that could deal with both the attack from the north and the British in New York City? What about Arnold's fleet? Can he hold back the assault upon us? What will happen to us if we fail? The prospect of becoming a prisoner on one of those old ship hulks is most frightening. 'Tis said the British prison wardens are selected for their cruelty and hatred of we colonials. Of course, there are no answers; only time can provide them.

October 12, 1776.

Today we could hear the heavy guns echoing from up the lake. The mountains to the west and east funnel the sound to us with the most ominous noise I've ever heard. The booming began late in the day and continued until 'twas dark. The orders came for us to make preparations to receive the British. We sit and wait yet again.

October 13, 1776

We were at our positions by 4:00 am the next morning and were afraid of what lay in store for us. The cannon fire began again around noon, and it seemed closer than what we could hear yesterday. They are coming for sure, and not just Redcoats but those barbarian German cousins of King George and the Indians. We have heard stories about the Hessians and how they are inhuman demons who would bayonet babies and take no prisoners.[30] We know what the Indians are capable of, as the old French war wasn't that long ago, but we are ready to defend our works to the last if need be. We have the numbers to give them a rather unpleasant greeting. But for now, more waiting.

October 15, 1776

Of course, we had no idea what was happening at the battle of Valcour Island (as it is being called) when it was going on, but today we had news from some of the survivors who tell a most exciting story of the battle on Lake Champlain. As the British moved down the lake towards us, Arnold had our fleet move to the New York side of Valcour Island. The enemy fleet sailed past the island without seeing our boats, and when Arnold gave the order to open fire, the British were most surprised. After an exchange and some shifting into position, they tried to bottle up our fleet in the island's narrows, but Arnold was much too clever to be trapped so easily and maneuvered between the British fleet during the night. He was heading south with a supporting tailwind when the wind shifted and began to favor the British. They soon made up for our fleet's head start and began to close in on our gunboats. Then, their longer guns took their toll and Arnold had to scuttle most of his boats. The fleet has nearly been destroyed; only five of the 16 vessels remain afloat. Wounded and parolees have begun arriving. Arnold and his crews received the camp's thanks for their "Gallant Defense," but the feeling of the men is one of fear and disbelief.[31]

October 17, 1776

News comes of a British camp at Chimney Point, a few miles up the lake. Their troops are reported to be moving up the Otter Creek. We were given rum and water rations at our battle stations. The men are nervous and fire at anything; a lot of shooting and shouting to our right resulted in one very scared, but still unharmed cow that had wandered too close to our lines. Later in the day, Baldwin and a detail of men began affixing a chain boom across the shores of both installations. A ship will find a most difficult passage through to Skenesboro.

October 20, 1776

The engineer, Colonel Baldwin, was observed today taking measurements and soundings from the lake between our shore battery and the Jersey battery over at Fort Ticonderoga. We watched and wondered what he was up to. The weather grows colder and the nights longer. Even when we are in our shelter, the wind find its way inside. What will it be like when winter truly arrives?

October 21, 1776

The men of the Second Brigade have been assigned to assist Colonel Baldwin in a detail of woodcutting. They are dragging large timbers from afar and tumbling them into the lake, where men in bateau are maneuvering them into position. It appears a bridge is being built to connect our two forts and further confound any ships foolish enough to attack. Happily, our brigade was not given the task, and we can spend the time watching the construction.

October 23, 1776

The bridge-building continues and is nearly complete. It is a most curious construction, having floating logs strapped to the boom with iron straps and held down by anchors. It bobs and weaves with the waves, and when it's windy, it rocks so as to dump a man into the lake if he's even the slightest bit unsteady. I doubt a man could carry much of a load across it safely, but when the need is to merely shift men back and forth, it should prove most adequate. Unfortunately, most days here do produce enough of a wind to make any crossing arduous.

October 25, 1776

At last some activity to write about. We have held these positions for the past week. Our legs are stiff and tired from sitting or standing, and we only leave the line in small groups to cook and eat our meals, which have been reduced to once a day. But, now, finally, there is some action to the north. Canoes were spotted at Three Mile Point yesterday, and the alarm was sounded. Before any attack could develop, Mother Nature got involved, sending high south winds that will keep the British from sailing towards us. These south winds will produce more rain and, by the time they die down, the chain boom and bridge will be now in place—with the bridge being completed earlier today. I say let them come now; their ships will foul in the chain, and our batteries will make short work of them.

October 27, 1776

Days of waiting, short rations, cold rain, frosty nights, and no British; no attack. We stay at our posts, endure, and wait.

October 28, 1776

It's been almost two weeks since Valcour Island, and our wait is over. Five British ships were seen unloading troops at Three Mile Point. General Gates ordered three regiments to man the old French Lines on the New York side. Two British vessels moved closer and were engaged by the Jersey Battery on the Ticonderoga side, and around sunset, they began to withdraw. Their attack has failed before it began! We've beaten them back! Now what will they do? Perhaps an attack from the Grant's side of the lake will be in order? Maybe they will regroup and try again? But still, we have defended ourselves successfully.

October 29, 1776

A wonderful day for our new nation and our troops! General Gates has sent this message to us as he sent his thanks to "the whole Army for the alert, and spirited manner for which they prepared to face the Enemy." We have repulsed the mighty British and turned them away. Our scouts report they have regrouped near Crown Point and will not return.

November 1, 1776

Finally, we've been moved back to our brigade cabins. Some 700 of our troops along with another larger group from Ticonderoga have been sent north to attack the Redcoats. Perhaps this will force them into responding in kind with an assault upon our works. After all our preparations and efforts, it will truly be a disappointment if we can't defend these forts. The sheer boredom of doing nothing but wait has everyone anxious about what is to be. It is the absolute worst part of soldiering I have yet to be part of.

November 8, 1776

Within a week, a force sent north to attack the British at Putnam's Creek found their rear guard had just departed. There will be no more fighting for the rest of 1776.[32] Now what is there to do? We have some time to serve before our enlistments are up. There will be no more assaults upon us until spring, and we certainly will not try to take Montreal again. By then I will be long gone from this frontier bastion somewhere near the ends of the earth. This isn't the Lake of Champlain! No, rather this is the River Styx, and all who are here have crossed over into the realm of Hades!

November 10, 1776

We are beginning our winter quarters here and have descended into a most mundane existence of fatigue duties. Wood crews, guard and picket duty, drills and marches. Rumors filter into the camp from the south, indicating Washington's army is nearly done for. Defeat after defeat has plagued our comrades, and they have been driven from New York into the Jerseys. We have heard General Howe now commands New York City. Stories abound of Washington's capture and the destruction of his forces. The rumors would have us believe the General has been sent to London for trial and execution. Despite this, few believe Washington is a prisoner of Billy Howe.

Our supplies are less than adequate as winter moves in and will probably get worse as the cold weather arrives in strength, especially considering the amount of people stationed here. So far, November has been rather mild with less rain than the months before. There have been mutterings that some of the forces here will be sent south to aide Washington's men. I truly hope Burall's is amongst those going, as I fear what will happen to those who remain here.

November 15, 1776

The rumor of units heading south to join Washington has been proven not to be a rumor, but fact. Hundreds of men from New England, Pennsylvania, and Yorker regiments have already left, some for Washington and others for their home states to guard against the enemy's attacks that are sure to come now that Billy Howe holds New York City. Alas, Burrall's is not amongst those leaving. We are stuck here on this peninsular mount of rock, this insignificant corner of Hades, this God-forsaken bastion of our revolution.

The lake is beginning to freeze over as the weather grows colder and colder. Winds from the northwest chill us to the bone during our drill, and it becomes difficult after only a short time to achieve our maneuvers. I cannot fathom how we will fare as the winter closes in upon us. I fear we are ill-prepared for what awaits us. Our supplies are dwindling. We have no spare clothing, nor blankets or overcoats to keep us warm. Our shoes, which we have worn since last summer almost daily, are rotting off our feet. Scarcely a good pair do we have between the five of us in this cabin. We share that pair when one of us draws guard or fatigue duties.

November 24, 1776

Flip has procured an old hide from one of our beeves and is attempting to make shoes of it for us all. He says we are lucky to have it and not to ask how he got it. We all take turns scraping the hair from the hide and rubbing salt into it in an attempt to make it pliable. As we have no way of curing it, we shall be wearing untanned leather upon our feet. Still, as our shoes fall apart, this should prove to be a most welcome alternative. We've been having flurries of snow on and off, and it shouldn't be long until we have our first real taste of winter.

November 26, 1776

We are finished with our new shoes; all five of us have a pair, and we have rawhide left over. In all honesty, it is folly to call them "shoes." Made from an odd-shaped single piece of hide, they are more like leather wraps, or more correctly, hide wraps about our feet. Almost Indian moccasin-like, we bind them to our feet with strips of rawhide run through holes punched into the leather and tied as tight as we can get them. It seems untanned leather does hold its shape as well as tanned leather, and by tying the smoother side towards our feet, they are almost comfortable. Our ragged socks, such as they are, help cushion the rawness of the leather from our skin. I'm sure some blisters may appear, but the alternative to what we would have otherwise makes a little rubbing manageable.

November 29, 1776

It's begun! Last night we received a steady fall of snow, depositing nearly ten inches upon the camps. As the day went on, out came the Sun and began soften the snow. All told, November has not been too bad for weather. Yes, it's gradually grown colder, and we did get our first snowfall, but nothing to make our lives more miserable than they already are.

Our new shoes have proved adequate against the elements, to a point. They fit well enough when dry but return to a different state when they become wet. And today proves it. With the melting, the snow saturates them when we walk in it, and the shoes become sloppy on our feet, resulting in a series of slips, slides, and spills as we attempt to cross our campsites. It soaks our threadbare socks, and our feet become dreadfully cold very quickly. Our only solution is to dry not only our shoes and socks before the fire, but also our feet. As winter has just begun, I know not what we shall do to prevent this from happening. Still, these shoes are better than going barefoot into the snow.

November 30, 1776

Eureka! A solution to our shoe problems has been delivered to us once again by an Oneida Indian. I don't know if he is the same one who saved me from my illness or not, but Flip has been given instructions and a bag of goose or bear grease. It stinks so as to drive us from our warm cabin into the night.

Yesterday we wet our shoes and covered them with ash from the fireplace then placed them before the fire to dry as we slept. This morning, we covered them with the Indian's grease and again set them to dry. When I wore mine out this evening, my feet remained dry despite the snow and mud around our huts. Now if only we had more clothing.

PART IV

WINTER, HOME,
& BACK AGAIN

December 2, 1776

It is now early December, and the British have been long gone. Since there is little chance of them returning before spring, more and more units have been transferred south. Our numbers here have dropped drastically since the enemy gave up the attack so many weeks ago. Now those of us who are left here are battling the beginnings of what promises to be a hard winter. Snow covers the ground everywhere to a depth of 10 to 12 inches.

December 10, 1776

The one-year enlistments for Pennsylvania and New Jersey regiments are up, and they've begun to depart for their homes. Others are still being sent by General Gates to help Washington's army near New York City. General Gates himself left in early December, and Colonel Wayne was placed in charge, much to our dismay. We would have much preferred a New England man, like John Stark, but he, too, was transferred south. Now, we are in for a rough time. Wayne prefers his Middle Colony men, and we New Englanders will become of lesser value.

December 15, 1776

Within a few weeks, the Northern Army has dwindled from nearly 13,000 under Gates to Colonel Wayne's new command, which contains just over 2,500 men. Burall's Regiment has to stay until early January; we five still share our shelter and take turns doing guard and wood duty. The weather had grown much colder, and the lake is nearly completely frozen. The wind howls out of the northwest with such fury as to freeze a man in his tracks. We filled all our cracked and split wooden planks in our cabin with mud a few weeks ago. Good thing, too, as all the mud is frozen as solid as rocks. We've considered moving into the barracks within the Star Fort, but they are still undone. They lack windows and doors, and truth be known, we have had little work done on them for some time. They'll probably not be finished until spring.

Supplies are dwindled; few new materials reach us. Snow falls have become more common, and we know it won't be long before deep snow covers the ground. There is not a lot to do, and we grow weary. We have insufficient food and clothing, except for our shoes, which are still holding up nicely. We find by adding more grease from time to time, they remain resistant to water. However, it is blanket and coats we need, as we have no coats to protect us from the biting wind and snow. Men are freezing to death in their sleep almost every night. Much of Burall's are sick or incapable of even the slightest activity on any given day. We are fortunate that our cabin has been cared for by all of us. We are healthy and are warmer than most.

Early December brought another change no one expected. Colonel Wayne ordered the Third New Jersey Regiment to move from Ticonderoga to Mt. Independence, where they are to occupy a departed regiment's shelters. These cabins have not been finished; some lack doors and floors and have open windows with no parchment or shutters. There is no way those men can stay warm through a night like the ones we've been having.

December 19, 1776

We are trying to make the best of a bad situation. However, what happened should have been expected, as those low-life Jersey men intruded into New England's space. It started out as name-calling but ended with fisticuffs. Their anger at having to leave the comfort of the old stone fort and real barracks for the cold, draughty wooden shelters was made worse by our presence. Many of us had been using the wood from those huts for firewood, despite orders to the contrary. But we had little regard for an order when we were freezing to death every night and the supply of firewood was miles away. Wood details are now dragging sleds of firewood across the valley from nearly four miles away. It is easier to dismantle an unused shelter.

However, in regard to the Jerseys, there is no way to avoid squabbling with them, as we shared the water supply and parade ground. Tensions grow even between our officers. You see, we New Englanders know our officers as friends and neighbors, not as something special as the Jerseys do. They refuse to take orders from our officers, saying they are "not proper officers." So we ignore their officer's orders, too. This is a most dangerous situation developing. I fear it shall be a long time for a resolution to this as neither side appears to be willing to back down.

December 21, 1776

Colonel Wayne has ordered all regiments to have their tailors repair the men's clothing. He has purchased thread from itinerate tailors and seamsters to do so. 'Tis such folly! How can anyone repair that which is a repair! Put patches onto the patches that hold the patches? I fear he is out of touch with our circumstances. What we truly need is new clothing, from smallclothes to uniforms, shoes, and coats. Blankets, too, would be nice. 'Tis doubtful we shall see them.

December 25, 1776

Christmas Day! We celebrated by marching and drilling on the ice of Lake Champlain. We of the Anglican persuasion managed to toast the Birth of Christ with a gill of rum and some wine after we settled in for the day. Honestly, most of the New England men are Puritans and don't celebrate Christmas. Indeed, most of them consider it a Papist holiday conjured up by the Catholic Church long ago to appease barbarian tribes in place of their winter solstice celebrations. I, myself, am a member of the Church of England and support the holy day. It brings back fond memories of my Connecticut childhood. Now I can't help but wonder how my parents and sisters are doing back in Connecticut. It has been months since I've heard anything from them. My only solace is the realization that Burall's will be going home within a few weeks.

December 26, 1776

Boxing Day! Yesterday, while we were drilling on the lake, a riot broke out between the Second Pennsylvania and the Sixth Massachusetts. It started when the two colonels began insulting each other and resulted in the Pennsylvanians firing 30-40 rounds into the cabins of the Sixth, many of whom were wounded. It came to an end when one of the Pennsylvanians produced a small, fat bear and invited the Bay Staters to dinner. Much as we despise the Jerseys, we don't want to have a similar situation erupt. So we both keep our distance from each other best we can.

Besides, we are almost due to go home; only about ten days to go. Our numbers are a fraction of what our strength was back in August and September, but the five of us are still holding on. Flip takes good care of us, using his rank to procure us as descent a ration as he can. Finn and I have become closer than brothers, as neither of us had one and could commiserate over having just sisters. Lewis Jerome is the slacker of the group and will try to weasel his way out of anything. Zeke Prentiss is quiet and constantly writing in his diary, too. But we five are ready to head out. Finn and I, turns out, don't live too far from one another back in the Redding area. We determined to keep up our friendship. Flip was looking to re-enlist, saying another regiment could use his expertise and maybe he could be a sergeant. Zeke just wants out. I swear, we—me, Finn, and Zeke—owe our lives to Lt. Trent because we got the pox treatment back last spring. So many died of that noxious disease here who could have been spared. Lewis is just too ornery to get any disease. Flip told us he was inoculated, too, because Trent had him and all his men done before the regiment first left for the Northern Army last January. Trent is now a captain and will be leading our group home; had it ever been revealed he had us inoculated against the pox, he would have been court martialed.

December 27, 1776

Snow began this morning sometime before we woke up. It's been snowing all day, and we have quite a bit on the ground. Our officers have ordered us to draw in extra firewood and rations and to stay inside till the snow ends.

December 28, 1776

Still snowing heavily, winds picking up. We sit in the dark to conserve our candles. Cold, hungry, and miserable we are.

December 30, 1776

The Nor'easter that hit us dumped more than two feet of snow and dropped the temperature to far below zero. For nearly two whole days, the wind howled like a dozen banshees; snow blew into our shelter through the cracks in the walls and threatened to douse our fire. The wood supply was getting low and we needed more, so we drew straws to see which two'd go out to the woodpile for more. Lewis and I drew short and slipped out the door as quickly as we could. The company pile was just a few yards away, and we made it through the swirling snow easily enough. Lewis loaded my arms full as he never liked to carry the heaviest amount. Filling me up would allow him to just carry what he could put on his own arms. I headed back as fast as I could move, as the snow was blinding in the approaching dusk. I practically fell through the door when Flip opened it to let me in and then slammed it shut against the freezing wind. Although we stood waiting by the door for quite some time, Lewis never came back. We found his body after the storm gave up earlier today about a hundred yards in the wrong direction. He must have become disoriented and froze to death during the gale. We buried him in a most shallow grave, as the ground is hard as the rocks below the soil. Even though Lewis was at times devious and tried to do as little as possible, he was still one of us and will be missed. Now we are down to four. Hopefully, the rest of us will get away from this death camp alive.

January 1, 1777

The New Year is upon us! Our nation celebrates its first new year. What fortunes or mishaps will 1777 bring to these 13 colonies? I can't help but wonder if this unification will ever work. It seems unlikely after what I have just witnessed.

Yesterday, our neighbors, the 3ʳᵈ New Jersey, dug a grave for two of their men who froze to death during the snowstorm. They built a fire upon the ground to soften the earth and went to retrieve the bodies of their comrades.

When they returned, they found the men of a Pennsylvania regiment taking advantage of their handiwork. They were in the process of covering their dead when the Jersey's returned. A scrap ensued between the two groups, which I must say we watched with some amusement, over the use of the grave. After some scuffling, the Jersey's prevailed, dug out the Pennsylvanian's bodies, placed their men in the hole, and covered them up. The Pennsylvanians took their dead over to a gully and covered them with logs and some rocks.

It seems folly to me to think our 13 states will ever get along after the display put on by those two regiments over their poor, fellow soldiers' bodies.

January 2, 1777

Our regiment has been asked to stay on an extra two weeks beyond our enlistment time. Almost to a man, we said "no." "Mad Anthony's" latest orders to drill daily on the lake have been met with venom and hatred by all stationed under his command. To think of spending two more weeks stomping up and down the ice is too much for anyone to take. We shall be leaving as scheduled, and Colonel Wayne and his ice marches be damned!

January 3, 1777

We have been ordered to stay, but we shall not obey that order. Our time is up, and we are mustering out. Wayne no longer has any say over our regiment. We are leaving on the morrow and may Mad Anthony rot!

January 4, 1777

The hour approaches for us to leave; fortunately, the weather has held. Captain Trent and Sergeant O'Toole will lead our company. We are leaving this corner of Hell before first light. By the time revile blows at 8:30, we shall be some miles away and happily so.

There are less than 50 of us mustering out. Our excitement is tempered by the challenges of the journey ahead. We gathered what belongings we could scrape together, along with some food, to get us started. Once we move out, there should be more game available. Perhaps the fishing will be as good as 'twas when we were heading for this place. Maybe we can catch some trout from that stream near Rutland.

Food and the weather will be our biggest concerns. The snow cover exceeds two feet in places, but the old Military Road has been used by sleds almost daily and is well packed down. We have built a makeshift sled out of some of our shelter boards, using the door from ours as the platform. We'll pile all our stuff on it and take turns pulling it along. I'm leaving with some anticipation, as I've heard nothing from the family for quite some time now. I fear something has happened to them in my absence; there have been reports and rumors coming from Connecticut that tell of troubles and Tory activity in the area.

January 7, 1777

We arrived at Rutland in just over two days and are camping back on our rise near the trout stream. The fort that was being built near the falls is nearly completed, and there appear to be more houses across the creek in what surely is the city. Most of the Otter Creek is frozen, but the little stream has some rapids that are flowing nicely, and trout has become our first meal of non-military rations. Another small snowstorm added to the cover, but the road is still fairly packed. Next, we move out onto the worst part of the journey—crossing the Green Mountains. Never an easy task even in the summer, it will take us nearly a week to get to the Connecticut River. We have some fish left from our efforts here and will haul them along. I doubt they will last long.

January 15, 1777

We arrived here at Number Four just yesterday, following a most exhausting trip. Even though we walked from first light to near darkness, the deep snow slowed us considerably. Wet clothes and shoes dragged us down, and cold feet and fingers were our nightly companions. A few of our men lost toes and fingers to frostbite, blackened by the cold. 'Twas a pitiful sight indeed to see these men laid low by exposure to the cold after surviving Mount Independence.

Game was scare, but a few snowshoe hares and a porcupine blundered into our muskets about a day after all our trout was gone. We arrived safely, although very tired and hungry, and were given a nice meal from the quartermaster's stocks. Medical attention was given to our frostbite victims. Supplies here are adequate, and we have been treated well and accosted by every sort of recruiter from every imaginable regiment in the Continental service with promises of rank, enlistment bounties, and free land after the war is over. Most of us aren't interested. Captain Trent has signed on as a major in the Third Continental Regiment of the Line; Sergeant O'Toole has joined with him and is now Lt. O'Toole. They are after Flip to join him, but Flip fears the Third Continentals will be sent south to help Washington, so he hasn't committed to anything yet. Our regiment has been disbanded, and we are all left to our own devices. One thing for sure, I'm going home. Finn and Zeke will be heading in the same direction since we don't live too far from one another. It's funny how we never knew of each other until we joined Burall's

Regiment, and now we are closer than brothers, each vowing to get together now that our part of the war is over.

January 21, 1777

Much to tell since my last entry. We mustered out at Fort Number Four and split up. Me, Finn, and Zeke stuck together after saying goodbye to Flip, who said he was going to hang around Number Four and re-enlist in another regiment.

The road was lightly covered with packed snow, but we didn't care. We were just happy to be home. Zeke was the first to split from us when we reached Fairfield County. He bid us well and took a right fork in the road to hang up his musket and live his life out "quietly farming", as he told us time and time again. He was the one of us who wanted no part of soldiering ever again. Finn and I decided we'd had enough, for now, but could come back for more. We were happy just to be almost home.

Finn and I walked another mile or two until we reached our ending point as a pair. We shook hands and promised to visit as often as possible, said our regrets, and went our separate ways. The houses along Black Rock Turnpike began to take on familiarity, but there were few of the citizenry about. Many turned away as I passed. It seemed most strange; although I was still far enough away from home and didn't really know these people, they looked menacingly at me. As I drew nearer, a feeling of dread came over me. I began moving more rapidly, keeping careful watch on my back, searching the shadows and roadside bushes for what, I didn't know.

Finally I neared my home. 'Twas ominously quiet. No one appeared to be there. I began to enter by the front door then felt I'd better not. Just as I began to back away, a hand was laid on my shoulder. Before I could yell, a familiar voice hushed me to silence. It was Finn! He motioned me towards the road, and we turned and ran as fast as we could before anyone noticed us. There was danger, but how and what I did not know. It was too late; we were being chased! I spun my head to look behind. There were three shadowy figures running after us and many more in the house. I had my musket, but it wasn't loaded: no bayonet, no tomahawk. Just a knife, but against how many? No chance for us. The road was still snow covered, making it hard for us to run; fortunately, it would prove likewise for any pursuers. Still, they seemed to be gaining. As we reached the end of my dooryard path, I heard a musket go off and knew we were being shot at. I instinctively ducked but kept running. I heard a scream behind me, turned, and looked to see one of my attackers clutching his belly and tumbling to the ground. The other two slowed, not knowing who or what had caused their crony's injury. Fearing more of the same, they dragged their friend back to my family's house.

It seems Finn's musket was loaded! He had outrun me and was kneeling behind a rail fence. He had fired a load of buck and ball. I joined him. What was he doing here? We slowly got up and began moving down the road, away from my parent's home. He told me he was heading to his home when he was stopped by a neighbor who told him that his family had been burned out by Loyalist sympathizers because Finn was serving with our regiment. His neighbor seemed very nervous and left after only a few words and gave no further information about his family. We headed back up the Pike, heading north towards Massachusetts. 'Twas then we decided to check on Zeke's place.

We were too late to do anything for poor Zeke. He had been executed by Loyalist "Cowboys" as a traitor to the King.[33] His father and mother and sister were left grieving. Zeke deserved better. Finn and I helped bury him and decided to head for Portsmouth, New Hampshire, where we believed there'd be more patriot sympathy. The Prentiss' were planning on staying on their farm but told us that many of those driven out by the Cowboys had headed that way. Maybe Finn and I will be lucky enough to find our families. Maybe we'll re-enlist and clean out Eastern Connecticut of the Loyalists. Maybe.

I'd served in Burall's Regiment for nine months, had witnessed deaths from disease and accidents, but had not myself fired a shot in anger. Neither had Finn until now, and I was mighty glad he chose today to do so. The last two days changed everything. I had no idea where my family was, although I was hoping Portsmouth. At least our property was still intact, and we might be able to reclaim it someday. Finn had lost contact with family as well as his home and farm. Zeke Prentiss was murdered for serving with us by a criminal element claiming to be true and loyal citizens of King George III. My world would never be the same. Nor would Finn's.

We got back to Fort Number Four to look for Flip and tell him about Zeke. Maybe we'd re-enlist with him in whatever regiment he'd joined, but when we got there, he was already gone. No one at the fort knew who he was and couldn't tell us where he went. We headed for Portsmouth and arrived here a few days later without further incident. Upon arrival, we had a little money but no place to stay. We didn't know anyone, and we looked out of place still wearing our ragged uniforms amongst the well-dressed city folks. Portsmouth was the largest city we'd ever been in, not counting Mt. Independence and Ti back a few months ago.

We decided upon victuals at a nearby tavern, having some continental script as our muster out, but we had no idea if the tavern would accept it. Everyone seemed to stare at us two scarecrows as we entered, and we took seats at a table a little away from the others and near the door, just in case. 'Twas then that a rather large, imposing man approached us, asking menacingly where we had served. His gruff demeanor softened when we told of our service in the Northern Army and our flight from Connecticut. Then he introduced himself as Colonel Pierse Long and said that he commanded a New Hampshire State Regiment.[34] Thinking at first we were deserters from Washington's army that had been soundly defeated around New York, the colonel seemed pleased we had served and offered us a chance to join his regiment as sergeants, telling us he needed men with experience to help train the others. We thanked Colonel Long and told him we were looking for our families but that we'd consider his offer. Long told us his regiment would not leave New Hampshire and by joining, not only could we look for our relatives, but we would be paid for doing it. Finn and I looked at each other and decided the deal was too good to pass up. Then Colonel Long bought us each an ale and told the tavern keeper whatever we wanted to eat was on him.

Colonel Long told us where to meet him tomorrow and arranged sleeping quarters for us at the tavern. We couldn't believe our good fortune. Us, sergeants! Hot food! A pint of ale! A room to sleep in that didn't leak, didn't have a dirt floor, and had real windows with glass instead of greased parchment—maybe even a real straw mattress! Sure, we'd serve again, but only in New Hampshire. Sounded like a good way to end out the war.

January 23, 1777

Long assigned us to Lieutenant Ezekiel Worthen's company, gave us a complete new set of smallclothes and a uniform, made us sergeants, and put us to the task of training his recruits to be soldiers, something we had knowledge of. These men had been with Long for a few months but were untrained and green. Seemed funny to be giving orders, but the men began to learn the drill quickly. We also helped with recruiting more men and were able to convince new enlistees to join with stories of the Mount and Ti, Arnold's fleet, the repulse of Carleton's attack, and the actions of the Cowboys. Finn and I quickly became celebrated as veteran soldiers, although neither of us had really seen any action, except our little encounter with the Cowboys.

January 24, 1777

Our ranks are growing as January wanes. The weather has been rather mild along the coast, and the food more than adequate. Portsmouth is a most pleasant seacoast town with wide streets neatly cobbled. Ships and supplies enter the port regularly, and whatever blockade the Royal Navy may have doesn't seem to have disrupted much commerce. Food is plentiful, much of it stored from the last fall's harvest, so we eat well. The meager meals and firecakes of the Mount are becoming distant memories. Taverns and shops abound, and the people are most friendly towards us soldiers. The Tory element of the city has either been run off or is keeping silent, and the majority of the population support the Rebel cause. We are quartered in some warehouses near the docks, so we aren't sleeping in the elements. We have traveled extensively around the Portsmouth area, but neither Finn nor I have had any news or contact with our missing families.

January 25, 1777

News from the south arrived today. Dr. Franklin has been sent in secret to France as our emissary. As it would seem, he went on board one of our warships and should have arrived there before this news comes to us. If anyone can help our cause through an alliance with the French, it's the good Doctor. His fame will precede him, and if the rumors of his charm and wit are as correct as I believe them to be, his successes in these pursuits will benefit our efforts perfectly.[35]

January 26, 1777

This is a week for good news! Today, we received the most magnificent news from Philadelphia. Washington has fought and won two battles in the space of less than a week, capturing a thousand Hessians and drubbing a force of Redcoats coming to their rescue. It seems the general was able to surprise the Hessians on Boxing Day and beat them before they even knew what was happening. It's said his army crossed the Delaware River in a snowstorm and took the enemy garrison at Trenton in the early morning. They captured over 1,000 of those Hessian Devils, along with their equipment and supplies. The Hessian plunder will serve Washington's army well. Then, Washington defeated a force near Princeton a few days later. We were told his army is doing well and has camped at Morristown in the Jerseys for the winter. It's the first good news we've had from the south since Boston fell nearly a year ago. Colonel Long led us all in drinking a toast to Washington and his men at our evening meal. Huzzah for General Washington!

January 26, 1777

'Twas about mid-morning when Colonel Long gathered us together for an announcement that shook us to the core. We are to move from our comfortable Portsmouth posting to Mount Independence and Fort Ticonderoga! An audible groan went through the room. Finn and I looked at each other in disbelief; we are going back! What fresh, new Hades awaits us there? We've scarcely been away but a few weeks, and now we're headed back. We are to move out the next day. And I've had no time at all to look for my family.

PART V

WINTER & SPRING

OF 1777

February 10, 1777

It took just a few weeks to reach the Mount. Worthen's company, our company, arrived first with 50 men sometime earlier this week. We kept good order, as Worthen later told Long, because Finn and I had trained the men so well and managed to keep order on the march. But 'twas not without mishap! My writing paper has been halved by the journey, much of it ruined by a mid-winter thaw, which, although providing us with warmer temperatures, also unleashed nature's fury in the guise of melted snow, fast running freshets, and torrents of mud. Much of my paper was soaked when my haversack slipped into a pool along with the rest of my belongings after a misstep along our trail. What I could salvage is still mud caked. But persevere we did, and we arrived ahead of the others.

Before long, the rest of the regiment trickled into camp in small groups. Colonel Long was most upset by this and found himself on the short end with Colonel Wayne, who told him we were an embarrassment to New Hampshire. This resulted in a promotion of sorts to me and Finn, who were named Special Sergeants in charge of training the entire regiment, not just Worthen's company.

We took our task to heart and began working the men with drill. The weather was cold; snow covered Burall's old camp, which we had previously occupied. The lake was frozen and made an excellent parade ground for marching, so we trained there. We were still well-equipped with decent shoes, uniforms, and blanket coats. Not so, our old nemesis the 3rd New Jersey, who were still stationed nearby but due to go home in early March. They looked even more ragged than Finn and I had when we'd first met Colonel Long and were less belligerent than before. Some of them recognized me and spoke to me, asking how and why I came back. They were amazed at my story and sympathetic to my plight with my family, promising to ask about them from their friends and family back in the Jerseys. We parted much more warmly than when they were first moved here from the Ticonderoga side. But they are now the ones going home.

February 14, 1777

The weather has been most foul since we've been here; bitter cold, swirling snowstorms along with freezing drizzle, drifting snow, and temperatures below zero for days on end all plagued us. Fortunately for us, Colonel Long has supplied and equipped us well. If we had remained in our old Burall's uniforms, we would have frozen to death, as they were nearly worn through when we'd left back in January. We were also lucky enough to all have shoes. Many of the other regiments here had few shoes among them and had to share when doing guard or wood duty. Quite a few of their garrisons are dying this winter; some from exposure, some of starvation, malnutrition, the pox, fevers, and any other of a number of maladies. There are daily new graves hacked into the frozen earth; some build cooking fires over the ground so as to soften it for grave digging.

Our supplies are low, and what arrives here is just a trickle compared to what was coming this past fall. We make do on much less and are encouraged to make soups and stews with what we get. Our meat ration is a fraction of what we should be getting. Dried beans and the like are only an occasional treat, and fresh greens are a memory. Even salt and vinegar are scarce. How often I think of Portsmouth and the bounty of plenty we had for oh-so-brief a time. How cruel is Fate!

We of Long's have suffered a few deaths but not as many as other units. I have come to the end of my writing paper, so this must be my last entry until another book or paper came be found.

Although my diary runs out here, I remember that winter as though 'twas yesterday. 'Twas abominably cold, windy, and snowy. Our rations were short, as food had to travel a long way to reach us. Game was scarce because 'twas long hunted out or driven further afield than we could travel. The lake was frozen and fouled with the slops of men stationed there since last summer, and to make matters worse, even the fish were scarce that winter.

We had to move farther and farther inland to get wood, dragging it on makeshift sleds back to our camps. Mostly we burned boards from abandoned huts and buildings, but this was against regulations, and we had to take care not to get caught.

'Twas never enough food to go around, and our meat rations were never up to standard. We often combed the old slaughter pits looking for bones that still held marrow, which we could free by splitting the bones and then add to our flour ration. Marrow on toasted firecakes sustained us many a frigid night. The good thing about the cold was it kept the weevils and other insects from the flour. But we also battled mice and rats for our share of the victuals. But oh, the cold!

The blankets we had to ward off the icy cold winter winds seemed more like cheesecloth than wool, but our plight was better than most of the men here. Still, between the blankets and the wood fire, which spit, sputtered, and went out at the most inopportune times, usually during the wee hours of the morn—we spent much of our time trying to keep warm.

As sergeants, one of my and Finn's jobs were to make sure the pickets were doing their duty and check them at their posts. Each man took a four-hour shift and was then relieved by one of their hut-mates. This kept the huts a little less crowded as there was almost always one man on duty. Still, 'twas a cold and miserable job for anyone during the long, cold, winter nights, but 'twas almost as hard a task for one of us to inspect them. Usually, we went alone, bundling up as much as we could with our uniform coats buttoned-up tight and our blankets wrapped around us. It took over an hour to check every man's assigned post. Through snowstorms, freezing drizzle, and biting winds, we'd go every night to make sure the camp was secure. Signs and countersigns were changed every day, and the pickets had orders to shoot at anyone not knowing or answering their challenge. But this was a rare occurrence, and guard duty was mostly just boredom. There was one story of a picket's challenge being rebuffed by a pompous officer that was regularly told around camp that I remember well.

Seems there was this lieutenant who was out of his quarters for some reason or other who, upon returning to our lines, had alerted a picket. The picket called out the sign "George" to which the countersign was "Washington." But the indignant lieutenant, his importance being offended by the guard, replied, "Ass!" to which the picket retorted, "Advance, Ass, and be recognized!" The story never failed to get a laugh when 'twas told to a group of soldiers.

As February waned, new orders arrived from Congress along with Colonel Baldwin, the engineer who had designed the defenses at the Mount. A new hospital was to be constructed. That meant more cursed wood parties venturing miles away to the forests, hacking down trees with dull axes, and dragging heavy, wood-laden sledges across the snow-covered fields. Still, 'twas better than marching on the ice of frozen Lake Champlain. This hospital was to replace an older one that had become dilapidated during the fall and winter. Prior to the building of this hospital, many of the really sick were being sent to a facility on Lake George, some distance away. Now the men could be cared for close by. The new one was to be much bigger, over 100 feet long, and would hold upwards of 500 men.[36]

While some men worked on the hospital, others began constructing two large bastions that would bolster the defenses of the picket fort. Built in two corners of the fort, these appeared to be similar to a blockhouse but with much more size and armaments. The work of these details fell to others, as we had been assigned to Baldwin's other spring project, building a bridge across the lake.

Baldwin! I swear, looking back on it now, he just wanted to keep us all busy and take our minds off the cold. He was, truly, a man possessed! Besides the hospital, bastions, and a bridge, he built a soap works and chandlery, a bake house, had men repairing store-houses that had sprung leaks or needed roofs repaired, and managed all that work and workmen himself. As soon as the weather warmed enough in April, he laid out gardens in the low areas along the lake shore. Next, he designed a crane to haul our supplies up over the cliffs from the bay below so as to deposit them near enough to the picket fort that men could carry them easily without having to load wagons and drive them up the hill. Baldwin had men constructing the base of this crane along the cliff top and others building a ramp and deck below by the bay where the boats could unload directly onto it. Then the boom would swing and lift everything to the upper level where most of the regimental quartermasters could access them.

The colonel would have nearly every man at the camps doing something. Cutting wood, sawing boards, splitting logs for beams and rafters, making shakes and shingles for roofs, drying parchment for windows, helping to build walls and floors, digging foundations and rolling stones to construct them, hauling kegs of nails and pitch, hanging doors… Whatever was needed to build what he was working on took up the bulk of our days and exhausted us as the day came to an end. Eating didn't seem as important as sleep, and I believe it took our minds off our gnawing, constant hunger.

During the winter, 'twas easy to shift supplies between the Mount and the Fort on the ice. The past summer 'twas much more difficult moving supplies back and forth because of the floating boom bridge. To help ease this, a new bridge was to be built to replace the old, floating one that kept breaking up and wasn't adequate for wagon travel. To our amazement, Colonel Baldwin was planning on building giant caissons, some of them nearly 30 feet tall on the ice between here and the Fort. Baldwin, who had calculated the depth the previous fall, made the cribs to fit the depths. He had us cut holes in the ice, and we began to build the framework right where they were supposed to be set for the bridge. Poles were set, as levers helped hold them in place until they gradually reached the bottom. Rocks were gathered and used to fill the cribs, some 22 of them, throughout the month of March. Men were hauling rocks from all over, using wagons or carts pulled by horses or oxen. Next, we'd load them into the crane's sling.

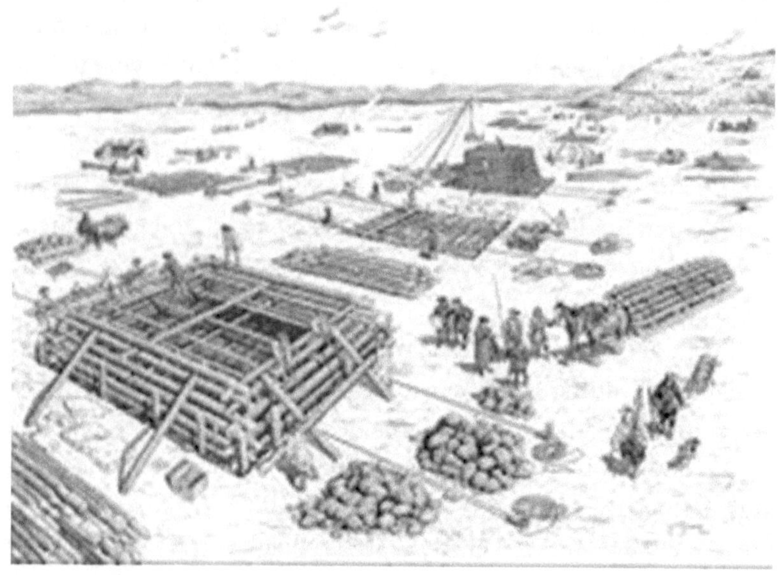

I spent many a day loading rocks into a crane and lowering them into a crib until they reached the top. Then we'd move on to the next crib and repeat the process. I never worried about running out of rocks, because if there was one thing we had an abundance of, 'twas rocks!

'Twas becoming warmer with the approach of spring, and the cribs nearest the center had ropes attached to them. The ice was becoming thin, rotten as we would say. Sometimes one of the cribs would split and topple over. Then we'd have to rebuild it and listen to Baldwin cursing nature and hard luck. But just as April was beginning, we made it across the lake. Nearly every able-bodied man and animal lent their muscle to the task of lowering the piers into the water as the ice melted. The ice was going out slowly, so nearly every day, we lowered a pier or two until we neared either shore. Planking the bridge would begin shortly after this.[37] This was the next task I was assigned to, and I spent most of April cutting boards in the sawmill to be used for the bridge's flooring. Then I got to help put them in place. The plan was that when we finished, a wagon could cross from the Mount to the fort over a sturdy bridge and still have room for a man to walk alongside. Not sure 'twas ever completely done.

With the arrival of spring, our supplies began to increase. More cattle came into camp, along with larger quantities of dried peas, beans, and lentils. Our rum ration returned. Baldwin's bake house supplied us with fresh breads almost daily. Now we even had cheese and chocolate on certain occasions. I can remember one meal of mutton that spring, a most welcome change from the beef ration. The regimental warehouses began to fill, and some of the more dilapidated ones were repaired for reuse.

Spring and warmer weather also brought more enemy activity. Towards the end of March, a group of our men were surprised on their way to Fort George from Ticonderoga. Gates responded with a 9:00 pm curfew and closed gates under guard.

Mad Anthony Wayne left us in late April upon the arrival of three newly arrived Massachusetts regiments. Massachusetts Brigadier General John Paterson replaced him. Most of us were glad to see Wayne go. He always showed favor towards his Middle Colony's men, those from Pennsylvania especially. However, now with the benefit of hindsight in my later years, Wayne was not so bad as we believed. Despite his ice marching orders, he did well for the post, keeping it in as good an order as he could considering the amount of soldiers he had at his command.

Also, old units left and new ones arrived throughout March and into April, but nothing even close to the amount of men that were there during the fall of 1776. A few of the militia units came to us in worse shape than we were ourselves; they came without musket, without equipment, without discipline, and above all, without food. Worst of all, outbreaks of disease either followed the men there or were lingering there awaiting fresh victims. Smallpox again, and measles hit us hard in late April just as the weather was warming nicely. It laid many of us low, and how I escaped it, I know not.

'Twas one of these new arrivals, Hale's 2nd New Hampshire Regiment, that gave me and Finn a grand surprise. Heading one of the arriving columns was Captain Eugene Johnson, our old cabin mate, Flip. I don't think he could quite believe Finn and I were back here. He promised us a celebration as soon as he got quartered in and told us of his luck enlisting in Hale's unit as a lieutenant and his recent promotion to captain due to the death of his predecessor from smallpox. We had plenty of stories to share. He asked if I was still writing, and I told him I had run out of paper. By our next meeting, he had procured an extra orderly book for me to use as a diary. I had forgotten how much I enjoyed writing in my dairy and was almost as glad for the book as I was to see Flip again.

May 10, 1777

Flip, Finn, and I are together again. Later in the evening, near the Star Fort, we shared some rum. Flip hadn't heard about Zeke and was mighty broken up when we told him what had happened. He had stayed at Fort Number Four just two days before signing up with Poor's. Said they'd made him a lieutenant right off because of his experience and ability to train men. Smallpox hit them a few weeks ago, and they'd lost many good men, including the captain he'd replaced. We told him our "Cowboys" story and how we got into Long's Regiment. As the hour was drawing late and duty called, we drank to Zeke's memory and made a solemn vow we'd always watch out for each other despite being in separate units. Flip said he'd keep us informed as to what was going on, as he was now an officer and privy to more information than we two.

With the approach of spring and the newly arriving regiments came a sobering thought. Campaign season was beginning, and our British friends to the north would be back. The old rumor mill began with the arrival of May and never stopped. We scarcely know what to believe. We heard that Governor General Carleton had amassed a force of 20,000 Redcoats and Hessians, escorted by 5,000 Indians, and was heading for Boston. General William Howe was ready to move his forces out of New York and attack Washington in his winter quarters near Morristown then turn north and attack our forts here. No, Carleton wasn't going to Boston; he, too, was heading for the Ticonderoga complex. Instead, Howe was moving to take Boston. Washington had been captured by a squad of British cavalry and executed. The Adams' and Jefferson had been taken to London for trial and execution. The rest of our Congress had been forced to plead for peace with King George. Which is true? What will happen to us? We are secure here in our fortress, but we lack men.

May 13, 1777

What a place! Just when we felt spring had really arrived, we got a snowstorm! We had about 3 inches of snowfall today. We'd had rain and some warm weather prior to this, but snow! In May? I have never been in a more fickle place for weather. If winter returned on the morrow, I would not be the least surprised. Ah, well, by the noon hour, much of it had melted, and as I sit and write this eve only traces remain in low lying areas and the shadows of rock. Mud now replaces the white carpet that was here this morning. Slips and spills accompany all who try to move fast across the camps. Such is our plight in this never-failing-to-amaze corner of Hades.

May 16, 1777

The weather now has turned dreadfully, devilishly hot! Our snow melted quickly, turning the grounds into short-lived mud flats; then the heat came and dried it to be as hard as the surrounding rocks. The wind blows from the south—what wind there is—and drags heavy, humid air with it. Even the slightest exertions result in heavy sweating and fatigue.

May 18, 1777

The Great Bridge is nearly complete. I have been on the planking detail all this day. It was ungodly hot, miserable work. The sun mercilessly pounded down upon our crew and never let up, reflecting off the lake as we crawled along, nailing board after board to the frame. What a difference this bridge will make in our work here. An entire wagon can cross from one side to the other. Now we won't have to shift supplies by hand.

May 20, 1777

Whitcomb's scouts are already reporting activity on the lake north of us. The British are indeed massing troops and equipment for a move up the lake towards us. Carleton turned his command over to another general most of us have never heard of, some dandy called "Gentleman Johnnie" Burgoyne. Some of the men said he'd been in Boston with Howe before they evacuated that city back in early '76. Scouts reported that Burgoyne had just returned to Canada in early May and was awaiting the arrival of the rest of his forces, which were most likely crossing the Atlantic in a convoy of troop and supply ships. How large a force would he amass, and how it would affect us? Could he dislodge us from our fortifications? Our position is most formidable, and we are prepared to defend it most intensely.

May 21, 1777

Colonel Enoch Poor and 600 New Hampshire Continentals arrived here yesterday. No untrained militia, they are most welcome. Colonel Poor is the senior regimental commander and will take over those duties from Colonel Patterson.

May 24, 1777

Still hot and miserable, but worse than that is what has happened to us here on the Mount. As I have written before, our garrison is small and composed of regular units like ours and continually arriving militia. Orders came today shifting all the regulars to the Ticonderoga side except for one. That one will keep tabs and work with the militias and will remain on the Grants' side. Of course, that regular regiment is Pierse Longs! Now we are stuck here with all these no account, thieving, indolent, undisciplined, untrained, insubordinate, useless boils on the bums of society whose greatest daily accomplishment is to see how much of the food supply they can consume. They are victual vampires to a man! I do not know why our regiment has drawn such a detestable duty, but I shall use all my power as a sergeant to make their lives miserable.

May 25, 1777

After more than a week, the heat has finally dissipated and in a most dramatic fashion. It was during the afternoon on this Sunday that the wind began to shift to the northwest. Along with that shift came cooler temperatures and, as the day progressed, higher gusting winds. By mid-afternoon, the wind was blowing so hard it broke the bridge and log boom from their moorings. Many of the men were dismissed from their church services to pull the bridge back together and make repairs.

May 26, 1777

We have been ordered by Colonel Long to train the militia, and both Finn and I have been relentless in our duties. They shall learn how to be soldiers, for if there is an attack upon us, all our lives will be in danger and all must endeavor his best to keep all safe. Oh, they grumble and complain, but they are learning. More of the same is scheduled for tomorrow. I am a hard taskmaster, and I am loath to say I enjoy it so.

May 29, 1777

Whitcomb's scouts have brought news of a large enemy force at Split Rock with two ships, seven gunboats, and forty bateau. They were firing cannons and muskets but did not advance any further. Perhaps a drilling exercise? Maybe just a show of force to intimidate us? I feel it is just a matter of time until they move upon us.

May 30, 1777

Now scouts report all quiet at Split Rock. Where have they gone? When will they be back? It is most unsettling to be awaiting immanent attack and have no knowledge of when it will occur. My fears and thoughts of the past October return as we once again prepare to receive the enemy. But I can't help but rationalize that we have an even stronger position than we had, with stronger works. The bridge makes it easier to shift troops and equipment so we should be able to fend off the British again. However, what we make up for in this area, we are lacking in manpower. We desperately need more troops to man the defense works, but where will they come from?

June 3, 1777

Many workmen have arrived here in the past few days, mostly bricklayers and masons with some shingle makers. It appears there will be a lot more construction going on despite the threat from the British. Although Baldwin's bridge is completed, the great hospital that he began in February has yet to be completed. It is a most energetic project and is larger than any of the other regimental hospitals in the camps. I shall not restate my feelings of our medical care once again, save to say the efforts being put into this structure may remedy many of the problems associated with the other hospitals here.

June 7, 1777

Another new arrival showed up at Mt. Independence. A young colonel and engineer from Poland, Thaddeus Kosciuszko, came to help design the defense. He was ordered here by General Gates. Colonel Baldwin is said to be upset about the new arrival and may be a little jealous. We have already heard much about an argument between the two engineers. Being just soldiers, we know little of the depth of disagreement between Baldwin and the Pole. But Flip filled us in on what he knew. It seems Kosciuszko suggested strengthening the breastworks and placing cannons atop the Sugar Loaf, which has just acquired the name Mt. Defiance, on the New York side. The argument that ensued between the two men was heated; both of them were adamant about their view and neither would budge. Just what we don't need right now is officers disagreeing with each other.

June 8, 1777

Today we had a big shakeup in our command. General Schuyler replaced Gates as Northern Commander and placed General Arthur St. Clair in command of the complex. In regards to fortifying the Sugar Loaf, General St. Clair quickly agreed with Baldwin and the matter was closed. It was said that St. Clair believed a goat couldn't climb Mt. Defiance so no one could ever get a cannon up there. Therefore, it would be a waste of time to try. Will this decision prove to be our undoing? Could the Pole be right?

June 10, 1777

So, it has been confirmed that the Polish Colonel's plan was defeated. Yesterday and today, he put us to work building a defensive work that is to protect the approach by the old Military Road. A series of blockhouses had been constructed along the top of the ridge. Now, we are adding a middle line of defensive works, along with a low, long stone wall that runs along the eastern perimeter of Mt. Independence all the way to the Star Fort and beyond. If the enemy lands on the eastern shore of the lake, they will have to contend with these works once they make it through the swamps that are part of the East Creek. It looks to be a most sturdy position and very well-planned by Colonel Kosciusko.

June 12, 1777

General St. Clair has sent his 12-year-old son back south to safety. He had come with him as a travel companion, but the danger of our situation has caused our commander to rethink his plans. All the troops on the Ticonderoga side have been arranged into four brigades by St. Clair, and they remain on that side of the lake. That still leaves us to be the only infantry unit on the Mount. Two Massachusetts militia units are under Colonel Long's command and are learning drill from Finn and me. They will remain with us until July when their enlistments are up. Flip's unit is at Ticonderoga, so we are not getting information as we did before, but I'm guessing there could not be a total of 4,000 men here.[38]

June 14, 1777

Some 700 of us are working on the middle line earthworks and building a most formidable position. All of the Negro soldiers and Indians from all the units here have been assigned to our work detail. Some of the men working with us don't like working alongside the Negros and Indians, but I don't mind. In fact, I can't help but wonder why these men were singled out for this duty except because of their color. Not that we couldn't use more help, but I feel a more fair distribution of workers could have been arranged. Most of these men are free men of color. Many of the Indians are Oneidas, who have supported our cause from the beginning. They are serving for the same reasons we all are: those ideals set forth in our Declaration. What will it take for this nation to live up to those ideals if we continue to own other human beings and separate them according to their color or religion? If I've learned nothing else after being stationed here, it just how much we all need each other in order to make the best of a difficult situation. It now matters less to me how a man looks as opposed to what he does.

June 15, 1777

More work on the southern defenses today. A row of blockhouses atop the plateau supports our long stone wall, and another stone fortification makes up the center. A powder magazine is near the center line, protected by a low-lying fold in the earth. Troops can shift easily between the two lower walls. Also, if one of our lines gives way, the retreating men will be covered by fire from the remaining layers. It should be completed very soon, since Kosciusko drives us as hard if not harder than Colonel Baldwin. He shouts at us in Polish and then French and still again in some variation of English when he gets angry. Sometimes, he gets a man who speaks French to translate for him to yell at us. I'm beginning to think all engineers are mad!

June 16, 1777

Work continues on the blockhouses, but most of the lower lines are completed. I'm tired and worn thin. The work is grueling, and all I wish now is sleep.

PART VI

BURGOYNE'S INVASION:
DEFENSE & EVACUATION OF
MOUNT INDEPENDENCE

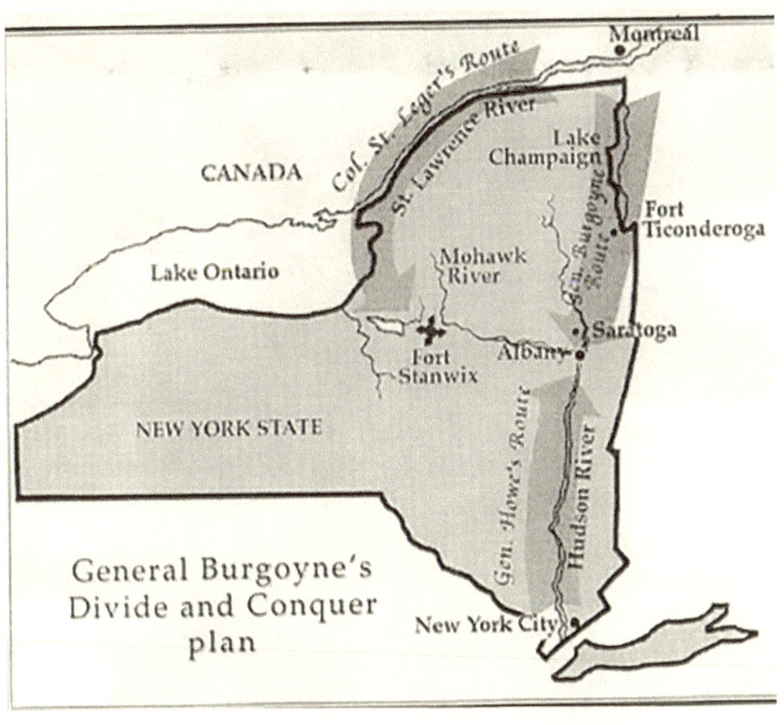

Montreal
Col. St. Leger's Route
St. Lawrence River
Lake Champaign
CANADA
Fort Ticonderoga
Gen. Burgoyne Route
Mohawk River
Lake Ontario
Saratoga
Fort Stanwix
Albany
NEW YORK STATE
Gen. Howe's Route
Hudson River
General Burgoyne's Divide and Conquer plan
New York City

June 19, 1777

We have lost men to advance parties of Indians who are near our outer defenses. Some have been captured, and we believe they have been sent to the British for information. Others have been scalped and mutilated, their bodies left for us to see. It is beginning to tell on the garrison. No one wishes to picket our lines for fear of being kidnapped by the Savages, so we have begun sending the men two at a time. Both Finn and I check on the details together so as to protect each other. It has also made our pickets nervous and trigger-happy. It has become a most dangerous duty.

June 21, 1777

Two days ago, we had four killed, three wounded, and two captured between Fort Ticonderoga and Crown Point. Two of the dead were killed just beyond the Old French Lines, part of the outer defenses of Ti. Yesterday, 30 Redcoats and some Indians were seen near Crown Point. Enemy activity is increasing. The alarm has been sounded, and the entire post is on alert. Yet, we are confident we can hold our positions against the enemy. Now, with the addition of the southern battery, we are even stronger.

June 28, 1777

Throughout June, we have heard reports of increasing British activity to the north. Attacks upon our men who venture out on the Ticonderoga side have been stepped-up; nine gunboats have been spotted along with a large number of bateau. Reports come in telling of a large encampment of tented regulars north of Crown Point.

June 29, 1777

Our biggest problem is the size of the garrison; we have less than 3,000 men, which is hardly enough to defend our works. We can't help but wonder what our officers will decide to do when the British move upon us.[39] *As June wanes, we get news of enemy vessels entering Cumberland Bay and that a smaller force has moved up the Otter Creek heading into the interior of the Hampshire Grants. This became confirmed when our scouts returned and described large numbers of British, German, Loyalists, and Indians at Putnam Point, and we were ordered to assist in moving all the provisions and powder from the Lake George landing to the storehouses on the Mount.*

June 30, 1777

Yesterday, we had reports of a force of Redcoats moving up the Otter Creek and heading towards Rutland to cut off our supplies coming from there. Hundreds of us have been moving all our foodstuffs, cases of wine, and barrels of rum, and now we are also removing all the powder and shot from the magazines at Fort Ti. It looks like our Star Fort on Mount Independence will be our bastion of defense. The amount of materials we have accumulated here already can sustain a garrison of our side for a couple of months. We are all anxious and ready to defend the Mount from all attacks. The enemy will find themselves facing a most determined foe.

July 1, 1777

During the last day of June, 18 British gunboats arrived at Three Mile Point and began disembarking troops on the New York side. About 300 of these made a move on the bridge but were driven off. That afternoon, two large warships moved up and formed a line across the lake with the gunboats. More troops arrived the next day in 40-some bateau and have landed on the east side of the lake. We are already outnumbered, but the arrival of a few militia companies added some reinforcements, such as they are. These militia units are always suspect; mostly, they are composed of a most cowardly element whose main concerns are their skin and their appetite. They devour our precious rations and are usually poorly trained and disciplined. They have a reputation for running in any action they see. We have little use or regards for them, but they're better than no troops at all. I know I've said this all before, but now, unfortunately, it's beginning to look like we'll have to rely on them very soon.

July 2, 1777

Yesterday, we were told of 40 bateau filled with Redcoats landing near Three Mile Point. There is no doubt as to where they are headed. We have heard reports of Hessian troops moving on us along the shores of the Hampshire Grants. If these rumors are true, we may be caught between two wings of Burgoyne's army and surrounded. Our escape route down the Military Road will be cut off by the Hessians while the British move south of us to control the water route to Skenesboro. We will be forced to fight them here.

July 3, 1777

Everything began to unravel on July 2nd. British troops reached our outer defenses just outside of Ticonderoga on Mt. Hope. Our men retreated to the Old French Lines near the fort. The British pursued, and we could hear the muskets firing back and forth, along with some artillery. Later, we were told nothing really came of it except a waste of powder.[40]

July 4, 1777

Finally, some time to write. This day should be full of celebration for our first year of Independence. However, everything here has been full of so much confusion and desperation. The reports are confirmed; we are in the process of being surrounded by the enemy. Our scouts report Redcoats moving upon us on the New York side and those Hessian devils closing in on the eastern shore of the lake. July 3rd brought us more reinforcements with the arrival of Colonel Bellow's New Hampshire Militia, 800 strong, along with some most welcome and yet sad news for me.

One of the officers sought me out to give me a letter from my mother. She and my sisters are well and living in New Jersey with a distant cousin. Father died from smallpox just before they were driven out of the Connecticut homestead. With Pa gone, my mother and sisters could put up but little resistance to the Loyalist "Cowboys" in the area and were quickly driven out. Ma was able to find me due to one of her cousin's neighbor's return from Mt. Independence with the 3rd New Jersey, who had remembered my story about the Cowboys and the search for my missing family. The letter made its way to New Hampshire via another neighbor's packet boat to one of Colonel Long's warehouses. There, 'twas given to Colonel Bellow, who knew he was heading to the Mount and that Long's Regiment was there.

I am amazed at this turn, delighted to hear from my mother and devastated by the loss of my father all at the same time. At least I know they are safe for now. Whenever I get away from this place again, I shall know where to find them.

We celebrated the Fourth with an artillery duel that lasted for hours but did little but waste more gunpowder. We showed them we are still here, a year after declaring ourselves free from British rule.

July 5, 1777

I find that I may have little time to grieve for my father, as this may be the day that seals our fate. We saw for ourselves the cannon the British have placed on Mt. Defiance, the Sugar Loaf. We could see the gunners moving about plainly. We watched as a shot from the Ticonderoga side crashed harmlessly below their position and as another fired from here did the same. Our situation now seems most perilous. I can't help but remember the argument between Baldwin and Kosciusko. I guess the Pole was right. The cannon definitely gives the advantage to the British. They can hit us easily from their position. Perhaps we shall have an artillery duel to drive them off as there appear to be only two guns on the summit.

So, for now we sit and wait. I am confident we will defend this bastion and repel the British. We are strong in our works, and I am told well-supplied. Camp rumor is that we have enough food and ammunition to hold out here for a month or more. I'm sure all will go well.

Still, my thoughts are with my mother and sisters, on their own since father's death. I hope they are safer than I at this moment.

July 6, 1777

Just a fast entry before we must go. Little did we know how perilous it was during the daylight hours of the 5th. We knew the British had already taken the Sugar Loaf. Now, they are moving on the outer defenses of Fort Ticonderoga. Their German troops are moving to cut off the old Military Road here on the Grant's side. It is only the swamps of East Creek that must be slowing them down. We're on the verge of being surrounded, cut off from retreat, and facing a long stay in one of His Majesty's prison hulks.

'Twas early in the evening when we heard of the decision to evacuate the Mount completely and under the cover of darkness. Shock! Dismay! Anger! We were going to just leave everything we had worked for to the British without firing a shot. Yet, still there was a sense of relief. And the idea that we'd be gone before the British even knew we had left was certainly appealing. I, myself, was beginning to wonder if I'd ever fire my musket in anger, or at all for that matter. We began packing our personal items, divvying up provisions, sorting out the regiment's stored goods, and getting ready to move throughout the evening of the 5th. Evacuation is to begin during the wee hours of this morning, July 6th.

My diary pages have this portion missing for reasons that should become apparent. I will recollect the actions of those confused days as best I can. The days that stretched from July 6 to July 9, 1777, when we were in retreat from Mount Independence, were the most harrowing of any I can remember. Also, there seems to be some other days of interest when I had no time to put thoughts on paper, so they, too, will be recollections.

Everything was going smoothly—too smoothly. Then around 1:00 or 1:30, it happened. A fire broke out in the cabin of the French dandy who commanded the First Brigade, which lit up the entire area like 'twas daytime.[41] Of course, now the British could see what was going on and that our troops were leaving the Mt. Independence defenses. It was just a matter of time before they'd be upon us. Panic set in. Many of the militia units lost their nerve and fled down the Military Road, causing blockages and jams. Officers screaming orders were ignored in their maddened rush to get away. The sick, wounded, and women and children were to be loaded into anything that would float and sent south to Skenesboro. Our detachment, Colonel Long's Regiment, was to be their escort and protection. All semblance of order ceased to exist. Soon there was no hope of getting away clean with all our provisions. Within an hour, most of the militia were long gone, Bellow's large group being one of the exceptions. The rest of the troops were to march south with orders to head for Castle Town, splitting from the Military Road onto the newer Hubbardton Road to get there. From Castle Town, they were to head west to Skenesboro, where they would meet up with our group, then south to Fort Ann and Fort Edward.

Finn and I got the men ready and we made it out in good order, clambering into bateau with as many men as we could cram into them. Despite losing everything we had constructed over the past year, we were getting away with our lives. On our way out, we saw Flip's command. He waved us over and told us that the Hale's 2nd New Hampshire was to be part of the rear guard along with Francis' 11th Massachusetts and Colonel Warner's Green Mountain Boys Regiment. He said Warner was in overall command of the rear guard, along with the walking wounded, and was in charge of the stragglers. We shook hands, wished each other well, and then Finn and I rejoined our charges. Many of the men complained of leaving the Mount and having to watch over women and children who had no business being at a military installation, grumbling at having to haul extra gear, bemoaning the fact they were running away from a fight. I had my doubts, too, but looking back, I see the wisdom in that decision. Nevertheless, the forts were abandoned by 4:00 am of the 6th of July, 1777. The British took them without firing a shot and were readying a hot pursuit of us. I remember taking one last look around at the place that had been my home for the better part of a year. Bathed in a wash of firelight from a still-burning cabin, I could see broken barrels of flour, peas, and beans lying hither, thither, and yon; papers strewn all across the roads and parade grounds and the litter of panicked men's personal belongings and equipment. I flushed with a feeling of remorse as I climbed into a bateau holding some invalided soldiers I was responsible for. We soon began our journey up the lake to the safety of Skenesboro.

'Twas a beautiful night for traveling up the lake; warm with a light breeze and a star-filled sky and no reason to hurry as we believed the bridge and log chain boom would keep the British from quick pursuit. We could hear the explosions as they thundered and echoed off the surrounding hillsides coming from behind us. We guessed the last ditch rear guard had blew the bridge so as to keep the British from easily taking the Mount. We broke out the Madera from the medical supplies, secure in our armada of five gunboats and dozens of bateau, and thoroughly enjoyed the journey.

We made Skenesboro in good time, entering East Bay just after noon on the 6th, maneuvered across the bay to the mouth of Wood Creek, and headed for the town docks of Skenesboro. We passed through the two steep hills that guarded the entrance to the little harbor and began to disembark, as we needed to make the short portage around a little falls. A small garrison of Scammell's Regiment met us. They had been stationed here to guard the town and knew nothing of our retreat from Ticonderoga. Colonel Long took command of them, sent all of our women, children, invalids and other non-combatants farther along up Wood Creek. The rest of us set to unloading the supplies for portage.

Then all Hades broke loose! With the docks full of provisions, the British began firing upon us from the cannon of their largest ship. Within minutes, the *Liberty*, *Gates*, and *Enterprise* had caught fire. Our other two craft, *Trumbull* and *Revenge*, struck their colors. We tried to form up against our attackers, but the militia amongst us broke and ran, seizing bateau, running into the woods or whatever they thought necessary in an attempt to get away. Then we grabbed what baggage we could and began our retreat towards the safety of Fort Ann, a few miles to the south. Panic became part of our retreat as shouts and warnings telling of Indians falling on the rear of our column pushed us faster. We had lost almost everything, including personal items and clothing. When we finally reached Fort Ann, we were sweaty, tired, and hungry, with nothing to eat. Needless to say, confusion reigned. Rumors that we were being surrounded by three British regiments and that their Indian allies were moving to cut us off were eased when Rensselaer's Militia joined us from Fort George.[42]

By the late evening of July 7th, we had regrouped. A small patrol from Scammell's ran into British pickets north of Fort Ann, and a short firefight developed. I had been in the army for over a year, plus a few months, and had yet to fire a shot at the enemy. Somehow, I had a feeling that would end soon.

July 9. 1777

At last, a respite and a chance to write of the past day's action. These days have seen us running for our very lives until yesterday. As luck would have it, this diary was in my haversack and not lost with my spare shirt and small-clothes. It seems to be only luck and providence that has delivered us to this day. But yesterday was my first firefight.

On the morning of the 8th, one of our spies returned with information as to the size of the British force opposing us. We had about 1,000 men; the British only around 200. A fierce thunderstorm rolled up, preventing reinforcements arriving to help support the Redcoats. After the storm let up, Long ordered an attack on the British left flank, and we crossed Wood Creek and began moving through the forest towards the enemy. It was the first time the regiment would go into action.

We began moving around the flank, and the British commander moved his men to a small hill in his rear. We poured volley after volley into them; they fought bravely for two hours, but by mid-afternoon, their fire was withering. Their ammunition had to be low. Then we heard it. A war-whoop shrieked in the distance. The Redcoats gave three cheers! Reinforcements had come for their rescue! And now we would have to deal with the Savages as well. Our ammunition was also growing short, so we began a retreat back to Fort Ann. The British held the field, but we felt we had been successful. We regained some captured men from the earlier Wood Creek docks fiasco and stood toe to toe with the Redcoats until their Indians and more soldiers came up. We moved back smartly and without panic. And I had seen my first action. Although I deliberately tried, I couldn't tell if I had shot anyone, but was myself unscathed.[43]

July, 11, 1777

More units began arriving at Fort Ann today, including the 2nd New Hampshire and Flip. He told us of his part in a battle at Hubbardton a few days before. His colonel, Nathan Hale, had been captured during the fight, and Colonel Francis was killed in the battle, but Flip said they nearly had the Redcoats beaten until the Hessians showed up just as they were about to turn the enemy's flank. Warner ordered a retreat, so they scrambled over a nearby ridge and disappeared into the mountains. Then they moved south to Rutland, regrouped, and headed here. So, since our leaving Mt. Independence, our forces have battled the British at Hubbardton and performed well against them, as did we at Fort Ann until the Indians arrived. Although we keep retreating, we have nothing to be ashamed of and are making this a fight the enemy couldn't have expected following our hurried exit from our fortresses.

Our Polish engineer has also returned to us from his travels. Together with Generals Schulyler and St. Clair, a strategy was worked out to stop the British advance upon us. It will be a most welcome thing, as we hear many reports of their Indians ravaging everything and everyone in their path. The local inhabitants are panicked with the thought of the Savages falling upon them and murdering them for plunder. They plead with us for protection and care not who we are fighting with or where our allegiances lay. Those who can have fled for points further south, Albany or Massachusetts, since the war seems to be heading in that direction and they are in the path of destruction.

July 15, 1777

The young engineer wants to attack Burgoyne's supply lines by destroying his ability to move needed materials to his men. Reasoning that everything must move from Montreal to his present position, Gentlemen Johnnie must keep a sizable force in his rear. From Ticonderoga to Skenesboro to Fort Ann and beyond, we will make movement most difficult. It takes a lot of wagons to supply such a large army, and when they reach us here in Fort Ann, they can no longer rely on using the lakes or Wood Creek. It makes perfect sense to us, and we are anxious to begin this plan of slowing down the enemy advance.

July 23, 1777

There has been little time to write, as we have been very busy with building a systematic trail of destruction from Fort Anne to Fort Edward some twelve miles to the south. We dropped dozens of trees all atop one another to create a tangled mass across the forested road. Clearing these trees alone would keep the Redcoat Pioneers working hard. So, in addition, we tore up bridges and flooded fields by diverting streams and ripping apart dams. Instead of dry roadbed, we turned the path into a muddy quagmire that would require re-diverting the water and putting down corduroy.[44] We can fell trees faster than the Redcoats can clear them, and their wagons should bog down in the muck created by our floods. We have turned the very wagons supplying our enemy into a liability for them and an asset for us.

With the Indians always in the back of our minds, we worked in groups, making sure someone was keeping watch. While we worked to destroy the path from Fort Ann to Fort Edward, the Indians fanned out in groups that scouted out our positions, sent reports back to Burgoyne, and terrorized the countryside. News of soldiers who were tortured and scalped came to us daily. Ambushes of work crews are becoming more and more common. Relief forces sent to protect workers are set upon and scalped, and their bodies desecrated. We have become powerless to stop them, and Burgoyne will soon whittle us way through these terrors or desertions.

The mutilated remains of soldiers are hung in trees, tied to fence posts, or displayed prominently for all the rest of us to see. Any unfortunate settlers who were in the path of these devils met horrible fates, as these Indians cared nothing for loyalty to any White man's cause but sought merely blood and plunder. Word has it that most of them are young braves from the tribe around the western lakes out to make a reputation in battle for themselves. We fear them more than the British or Hessians and know they cannot be trusted or controlled. No one is safe, be they Tory, Rebel, or apothem. Indeed, the countryside flees before Burgoyne's advance because of them. How we will stop them makes one ponder as to a solution, and there is no easy answer.

PART VII

SARATOGA

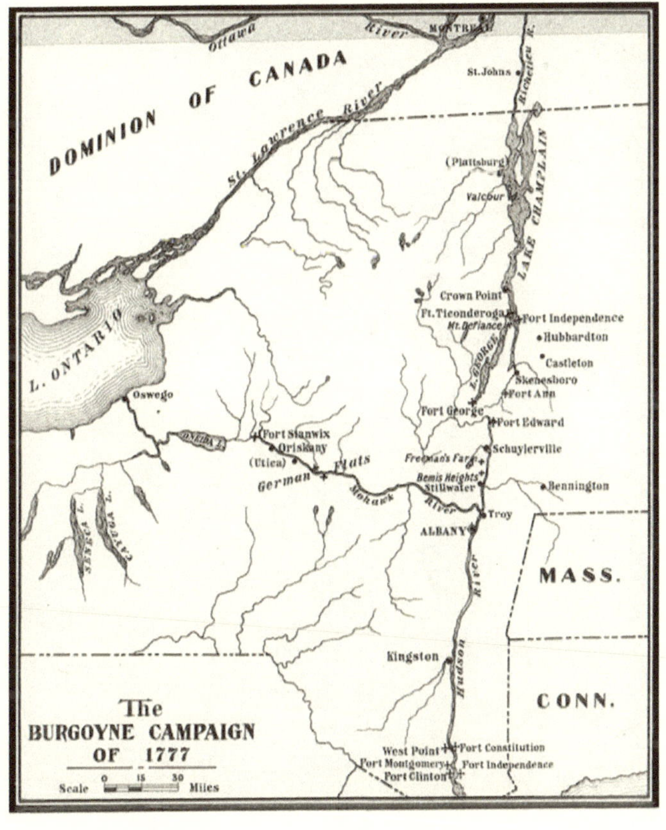

July 27, 1777

When we arrived here at Fort Edward, we discovered the bodies of ten men who had been scalped and mutilated by British Indians. We began to give them a decent burial when a most frightened Black slave appeared with news of the deaths of his master and family. Finn and I tried to calm the man to no avail. We were talking with him outside the fort. He was insistent on returning to his master's farm and taking us with him, and we worked hard on convincing him otherwise. 'Twas then we heard a ruckus and dove into nearby undergrowth. A party of Indians moving north up the main road soon met with another group coming from another direction. With the first group was a long-haired, redheaded White woman, seeming very comfortable with her escort. She was accompanied by another older, heavy-set White woman. The two groups of Indians began menacing each other. Words exchanged between the groups sounded angry, even though none of us spoke the language. Fear began to show itself on the faces of the white women. Now two of the Indians were shouting at each other, pointing at themselves and the younger White woman. Just then, one of the Indians from the first group turned with a look of disgust away from his opposition, paused a few seconds, got this look of abject foulness on his face, and shot the young woman in the chest dead! The older woman screamed, and the shooter slapped her across the face. He spoke some words to the second group, and the situation calmed down. He then took his scalping knife and removed the red hair from the corpse.

But that wasn't enough. He removed the clothing from her and began to mutilate her body. The whole time, the older White woman shrieked in terror for her life. After a bit, the Indian rolled the corpse down a small hill into a gully. He then grabbed his prize scalp, dragged the older woman up by her hair, and they all began moving north towards Fort Ann. What a horrible spectacle we were subjected to, but we remained quiet, lest a similar fate await us. That poor young women murdered and her body defiled, and we could not lift a hand to save her.[45]

Then 'twas over. The Indians left with their hair prize and the older woman, who by now was a whimpering, blubbering burden to her captors. But they seemed bent on taking her with them alive. We headed for the safety of the fort as quickly as we could with the slave alongside us.

July, 28, 1777

The murder we witnessed yesterday has begun to have great consequences. It seems the entire countryside has been buzzing with the news of this young woman's murder. It turns out her name was Jane McCrae, and she was the fiancée of a Loyalist who is serving with the advancing British army! If loyal British subjects are not safe, who is?

Panic has settled upon us all. Word spreads fast throughout the area. Many have already joined us here at Fort Edward, and I expect many more to follow. The slave has attached himself to me and Finn and has a most personable nature. His name is Quentin, and he was the property of a Dutch family named the Van Impes who were slaughtered by the Indians. He claims he had just gone to the barn to fetch another tool when he heard his master scream and saw two Indians smash in his skull with a war club. Before he could move, two more of the Savages came out of the house, carrying the bloody scalps of Mrs. Van Impe and the children. He told us he jumped into a pile of hay and covered up as best he could, but the Indians must have been happy with their prizes and left without searching the barn. After hiding for a while, he left for the safety of the fort and then ran into us.

He has no one to return to since his master is gone. He claims his master was a Loyalist, and he's too scared of the Indians to go back there. His master believed that since he was a loyal citizen of the crown, he'd have nothing to fear from the advancing British forces. Furthermore, Quentin feared he would be blamed for his master's death. He is nervous and still scared, and who could blame him? After witnessing so many murders in such a short period of time, anyone with his wits about him would be quaking in their shoes.

Now he is willing to serve with us if it brings him his freedom, so we've made him a part of the regiment. He's taken the last name of Freedman, so he's now Quentin Freedman, soldier. But Long's has only a short time left to serve before mustering out, and I can't say I will miss being a soldier after our narrow escape from Burgoyne's army. I look forward to returning to Portsmouth and maybe on to the Jerseys, hopefully to make contact with my mother and sisters. I only need to survive this ordeal.

July 31, 1777

We have left Fort Edward and are moving south into the Hudson River Valley. The fort has become a much more dangerous place to be, as the British are finally nearing there. Indian atrocities are on the rise, with many families murdered in the area since McCrae's death a few days ago. Rumors abound that General William Howe is going to come north from New York City to join Burgoyne in Albany, thereby cutting our nation in two.[46] This part of New York is different from what lies north of Fort Edward. It's mostly open land and farms, small hamlets, and rolling hills. It is much easier to move through, and when the British finally arrive, they won't be slowed by the mess we created for them south of Fort Ann. But oh, how effective our mess! It took Burgoyne nearly three weeks to move twelve or so miles. Still, I won't miss the back-breaking work of toppling trees.

August 3, 1777

We have arrived safely at Stillwater, New York after three days of burning crops and driving livestock before us. There was little opposition to our destructive practices because everyone is too scared of Burgoyne's Indians and have fled in terror before his advance. But we left little or nothing to make his march easy. No food and no peace of mind while his supply lines grow daily longer and thinner. His men must be demoralized, as his force dwindles ever so much with every fort he must garrison in order to feed his men.

August 4, 1777

I worry but take comfort in our time ending on the morrow. Soon, I will be out of this army and safe. And I will get new clothes and be able to change them and clean them instead of wearing the same pants, smallclothing, and coat day after day. My once new coat has become a non-shade of the blue it originally was, caked with dust, sweat, blood, and grease. It's been shot at, ripped by thorns and briars, splattered with all sorts of liquid matter, and generally abused in a most dreadful manner. It's torn and tattered, patched with pieces of a non-shade of any color I could find, all of which are sewn on as best as my stiffly nimble fingers could wield the needle. I've worn it proudly since January and will be loathe losing it. But I can't wait to rid myself of the piece.

August 5, 1777

Pierse Long's Regiment is going home. They muster out today and are finished with their terms of enlistment. Seems like years rather than eight months! I was ready to get out of this trap and to relative safety back in New Hampshire. Then, a surprise from Finn: he's not leaving the army just yet. Quentin agrees with him; they say we have to stick with Flip until this thing is over. I cannot fathom what I did. I must say, they were most persuasive, and I found myself relenting and agreeing to stay as well. We caught up with Flip and joined his command. He was most glad to have us alongside again, and Quentin, too. I can't believe I am staying, but these men are closer than my family. No, rather they have been my family for these many months. This is the only life I know. To not be in this army seems a difficult task, as I have forgotten how to be a civilian.

August 6, 1777

I've received some smallclothes and a coat from the regiment's stocks and have taken on a military air once again rather than resembling a scarecrow. Actually, I think most scarecrows would have been better dressed than I prior *to my new acquisitions! The coat is almost new, and I believe it belonged to someone else before me. Still, it is in good shape and a welcome replacement. It's even harder to believe that this is the third regiment I've belonged to. First Burrall's, then Long's, and now Hale's 2nd New Hampshire. I truly hope this will be my last and this war will end soon and I will reunite with my mother and sisters.*

August 8, 1777

Word comes to us of a battle to the west, in the center of what has been Iroquois country. A large force of Loyalists and their Indian allies ambushed a group of New Yorkers moving west to try and stop yet another group heading in that direction. It was Indian against Indian, Continentals versus Loyalists, and everyone fighting forest-style, leaving scores dead and wounded. Neither side secured a victory, although the Loyalists did leave the field.[47] *We have heard this force has also laid siege to our works at Fort Stanwix. Is there more to be heard from this British force? Will this become yet another threat to our forces here at Stillwater?*

The Iroquois have been broken by this fight. Some of them support us, notably the Oneida, such as the one who saved me when I was sick last fall. Others, like the Mohawk, help the British. These Indians have had an alliance with one another long before the White man came, and this war has destroyed it.[48] *What a war! We fight not only our King and government but also old friends and neighbors. Men we knew and worked with now try to kill us, as we do them. Savages slaughter indiscriminately whomsoever their path crosses. Indians who have had stronger ties to one another than any European nation I know about are now at each other's throats. The world will never be the same as a result of the turmoil we have created in our quest for freedom and independence.*

August 12, 1777

Little to do here but wait. We're building some stout defenses atop a height overlooking Hudson's River. Our forces swell daily. Some men have arrived from Washington's army to help here, most notably Glover's Marblehead fishermen, 1,200 men strong, about whom we all have heard great tales.

'Twas Glover's men who saved Washington's army at Long Island and rowed the general and his troops across the Delaware for the attack on Trenton last December's Boxing Day. 'Tis said they then took the vanguard during the attack after working and marching all night. With men like these, how can we lose?

However, along with units like Glover's come the militias. They are pouring into our camps daily from all across our region. Many who are with the militia say they are most disturbed about Burgoyne's Indians and especially the McCrae murder. Indeed, some of these units have had running battles with the Indians just to get here and have lost many of their members as a result. As soldiers, they are most useless, as they have no training and cannot properly fight. It is a gamble to put them in a skirmish line, as they may break and run after the first volley and have no knowledge of the bayonet. But they can dig with the best of us, load and teamster wagons, haul our supplies and ammunition, and minister the sick and wounded. For these reasons, we'll gladly take any and all of them.

Many of the Loyalists in the area are having a change of heart because of the Indian issue, too. We have heard through our spies that most of Burgoyne's Indians have gone home because he wanted to punish the Savages who killed Jane McCrae. Seems no one wants those Red-Devils around again. It is apparent the murder of that poor, innocent woman has had many repercussions.[49]

August 15, 1777

The weather remains hot as summer reaches its "Dog Days." Strange news reached us from the Hampshire Grants; yet again, another upheaval in the norm. Seems the Grants have declared their independence from all allegiances save their own. Meeting in a tavern in the town of Windsor, representatives from the Grant's communities voted to adopt a new constitution and declare themselves free of ties to both New Hampshire and New York or the British crown. They are calling their new colony Verdmont and claim themselves to be a free and independent state.

We have had experiences with Warner's regiment from the Grants, the so-called Green Mountain Rangers, and found them to be the most self-assured, reticent, and independent-minded men we've encountered. Yet they were involved in our cause. They provided soldiers for the defenses at Mount Independence. Warner's men covered the retreat from there and fought valiantly at Hubbardton. And 'twas their leader, Ethan Allen, along with our Arnold, who planned and carried out the capture of Fort Ticonderoga and Crown Point just weeks after Lexington and Concord. Although they are not with us here, they are a most daunting foe on the British eastern flank. Still, a bold move for such a small colony.[50]

August 16, 1777

Stillwater has become a formidable post. The heights near the town are fortified, again with the help of the Kosciusko, our Polish engineer who has been with us since the retreat from Ticonderoga. We have had little in the way of attacks by the Savages in the past few days, and even newly arriving militia units have come in unscathed. Perhaps the rumor was true, and the Indians have returned to their homes, or perhaps we are too powerful for them to attack as they prefer not to assault fortified positions.

General Schuyler has a home nearby, just north of here near Hudson's River crossing along the Albany Road. It is his summer mansion, so we are told. As a Yorker, he was one of the major landholders in this area, along with the Tory, Phillip Skene, who is now helping Burgoyne. What a strange war this has become when men of wealth like Skene and Schuyler concern themselves with property and money rather than the fates of the people who occupy their lands. I can't help but think of my mother and sisters and how they are faring in New Jersey. Or what's to become or has become of our farm in Connecticut. What will be left when this war is over? Who will be the victor, and will anything return to as it once was? Perhaps the scars between Tory and us revolutionaries will be a long time in healing. Whatever happens, we're dug in here, and Burgoyne continues to move south towards us.

August 18, 1777

The most astounding event has occurred to further help our cause. A sizable force of British and Germans have been defeated at Hoosic and Walloomsac River, near the town of Bennington in the old Hampshire Grants. It seems

John Stark, the old commander of the First Brigade at Mt. Independence, and Warner's Green Mountain Boys took out nearly 1,500 of an expedition Burgoyne sent to find supplies and horses. Most of those men were captured and now languish in the common houses of the town of Bennington. A most dreadful turn for "Gentleman Johnnie", and one he can ill afford as our ranks still continue to swell.[51]

August 19, 1777

Arnold has left us for the area of Fort Stanwix, where the British are besieging the small Continental garrison serving there. Once the enemy takes the fort, they will be able to move upon us with no opposition. But Arnold will stop them!

August 23, 1777

At long last, General Schuyler has been replaced by General Gates, much to our pleasure. Even though he's a former Britisher, we prefer him over Schuyler the Yorker. I can't help but wonder how Arnold will feel about this. So much intrigue amongst the general officers. Flip fills us in with what he hears and leaves us wondering what will become of this army as the summer continues.

August 24, 1777

A waiting game has developed between us and the enemy. We have continually harassed Burgoyne's movement. He is low on supplies; his cavalry lack horses; his numbers keep dwindling. Still, he persists. The force to the west of us is a continual problem. Rumors in camp have Generals Howe or Clinton leading a force north from New York City against us to relieve the pressure on Burgoyne. If this is so, it hasn't happened as of today's writing.

We here spend our time drilling. Our supplies are adequate, although we never seem to have enough food, which seems to be a universal complaint of every soldier I have ever met and probably has been the bane of every military man since the days of Alexander and Caesar's men before us! We, in our regiment, have been issued bayonets for all to use and have been getting training from some of the units arriving from Washington's army to help us. If it comes down to using it, I wonder if I'll be able to really run another human through. No army is better with them than the British, and the Hessians are a close second. How will I ever be able to compete?

August 26, 1777

Arnold has done it yet again! He managed somehow to convince the British Indians to go home. The British force lifted the siege and retreated to the safety of the Niagara frontier.[52] There has never been a general in this army with better abilities than our Connecticut's Arnold. When this war is over, he will be a legend and hero to our new nation.

August 31, 1777

New arrivals yesterday from Washington's army. A most formidable group of men than we have ever had have come to us here. Flip said they were with Arnold at Quebec City a few years back and that they would be a most powerful addition to our ranks. Of course, it's Daniel Morgan's Riflemen to whom I refer. These men are from the frontier of Pennsylvania and Virginia and carry the famous Long Rifle. Their prowess with these weapons have made them legends amongst our troops and strike fear into every living thing facing them. These are powerful, long-range rifles that can outdistance any musket I've ever heard of—Brown Bess, Charleville, or Committee of Safety—none of these come close to equaling the range Morgan's men can shoot. Clad in buckskin or linen "hunting shirt", these men are often bearded, boisterous, and loud, eschew military discipline, except where Daniel Morgan is involved, and will follow him to the Gates of Hell if asked by him to do so. It's also apparent that they believe in General Arnold, as they've attached themselves to his command before being assigned anywhere. Arnold and Morgan are "thick as thieves" and came to that arrangement during the Quebec campaign. I can't help but wonder what they'll do to Burgoyne when they get the chance. Finn seems most taken by these men and spends quite a bit of his time in their camp. He wants to learn how to use a rifle and, I think, aspires to be one of them.

Meantime, we still sit here at Stillwater while the British fritter their time away at Fort Edward. Supplies must be getting low, and what they are getting has to come all the way from Montreal, through the series of forts from Ticonderoga to Edward. Our scouts report numerous attacks and harassing of their supply trains. Must be a most unpleasant duty for the teamsters and waggoneers.

September 5, 1777

It's well into September, and the weather has the feeling of autumn. Burgoyne is still at Fort Edward, and we're wondering if he'll ever move upon us. Rumors abound that General Sir Lord William Howe has abandoned Burgoyne and actually moved south to attack Philadelphia and capture our Congress that meets there. When we first heard this, we thought 'twas madness. No British general would be that rash and abandon his own troops in the field. But Flip confirmed it the other evening, following one of his officer's meeting. Howe did indeed depart New York for Philadelphia with the bulk of the troops stationed there. That would leave General Clinton in New York with a small contingent and probably not enough to mount a rescue attempt. The enemy's navy won't be able to help as long as we still garrison Hudson's River at West Point. They cannot get past that installation and continue to transport troops up river to Albany. What will "Gentleman Johnnie" do now? Can he hold out until spring and the chance of reinforcements? Will Clinton come to his aid with a small force? Will Burgoyne try to break through our defenses and meet Clinton at Albany? All we can do here is wait.

September 8, 1777

Yesterday we moved north of Stillwater to the heights of Bemis and began fortifications. Led by Kosciusko and Arnold, we began to build breastworks and emplacements for our artillery. We can see the wisdom of this position, as it overlooks the Albany Road and squeezes near enough to it so as to make it uncomfortable for anyone trying to go by. Burgoyne will not be able to ignore us here. There is a small stream nearby that separates this hill, called Bemis Heights, from the line. Here is where our flank rests. Our ranks still grow, mostly militia, and we spend our time training them when they're not doing other more mundane duties. Let us hope we either don't have to rely upon them too much or they've learned their lessons well.

September 10, 1777

How we fret away the hours, days until the next movement. Armies are great for wasting a man's time. Our defenses are stout and well prepared; our militia now has had some training and seems ready to fight. Washington has sent us General Israel Putnam, who has a way with militia troops, so we're told. We all hope this to be most true, as we may need to rely upon them. I've seen firsthand the performance of militia during the evacuation of the Mount and at Skenesboro and realize that in this situation, their performance may be critical to our cause. Still, they are invaluable in the work they provide so as to free a regular for his military duties.

September 15, 1777

Burgoyne is on the move. Scouts report he crossed Hudson's River near General Schuyler's mansion and is now on the same side of the river as we. He'll soon begin sending his scouts towards us. I fear we shall be engaged with them very soon. I only hope I can stand with my comrades and give a good account of myself when the time comes.

September 18, 1777

I write this evening with a feeling of dread. Some nearby firing this afternoon made it clear the enemy had engaged our pickets somewhere close to our lines. Tomorrow or the next day shall be the day we meet the British on the field of battle. I have only been in the one firefight a few weeks ago at Fort Ann. That was a minor scrape compared to what we are getting into. May my courage remain steadfast no matter what happens. It will be difficult to sleep tonight.

September 20, 1777

Yesterday was a most magnificent day of victory for our cause! We gave the enemy his just do, and I must say I was able to give good account of myself and that our unit performed wonderfully. I shall try to capture the mood and feelings of the fight, but it shall be difficult to render perfectly.

The morning dawned most foggy and held up the British attack until noon. We could see from our position that their army was divided into three columns;

one alongside the river, another moving down the Albany Road, and the third heading just west of the road, making for our flanks here on the heights of Bemis. It was just a short time later that General Arnold appeared, and he ordered Morgan's Riflemen downhill towards the edge of the woods near a small farmhouse. We were to follow them and take a position on their flank. As we were moving into place, the riflemen delivered a volley that dropped every Redcoat officer I could see to the ground. Panic hit the remainder, and they began to break with Morgan's men pursuing them. Then more British officers arrived and rallied their troops for a counterattack, which sent Morgan's corps back towards our position. We waited until they were within 50 yards and opened fire. By then, Morgan's men had reloaded and they joined in, again dropping officers right and left, choosing their targets at ridiculously long distances. Still, the British came on.

Arnold ordered up more and more of our troops, and the fighting continued throughout the afternoon. Even some Connecticut militia units took part and gave good account of themselves. The fighting lasted three, maybe four, hours and ended when General Arnold could no longer procure reinforcements from General Gates and the Hessians moved some artillery pieces onto the field. For a short period of time, these cannon came under Morgan's fire and many of their cannoneers went down as they tried to tend their pieces. But our ammunition was beginning to run low, so we withdrew to our old positions along the heights of Bemis, leaving the field to the enemy. Although we took casualties, more of the enemy were lost to our actions to make this a most costly victory for them.[53]

I gave a good account of myself, as did Finn and Quentin. We fought alongside each other all afternoon and could see Flip moving his men and spurring them on while he, too, fired into the enemy's ranks. Today, we rest. Last night, the pitiful cries of the wounded and the cold lent poor sleep. Hopefully, tonight will be better.

September 21, 1777

Last night fared worse than the night before. Still the wounded lie unattended, and now their cries are accompanied by the howls of wolves that, I'm sure, are attacking these poor, helpless victims. Where are Burgoyne's men?

Why don't they come and get their wounded? Such folly! And why haven't they again moved upon us? It has been two days since our last engagement; surely they have regrouped by now.[54]

September 24, 1777

Still we sit, waiting. News comes from Flip concerning a matter of grave importance to our command. Arnold has been relieved of duty by General Gates and ordered to leave camp. As it seems, Gates' letter to his friends in Congress never mentioned Arnold's role in our last battle, and Arnold, true to his nature, took exception to the slight. Words were exchanged, and Arnold came out of the scrap under house arrest in his tent. Flip says the officers have signed a petition to have Arnold restored to his former command, but until then, we have been placed under General Lincoln. These officers are more like children and always seem to be embroiled in some sort of political intrigue against each other. How we will ever become a country under these conditions eludes me![55]

September 26, 1777

Word has come to us of an assault upon the works of Fort Ticonderoga and Mt. Independence, now held by the British, by a sizable force of our troops led by Colonel John Brown. A most bold move by our forces! This should push the enemy into making a move. As it would seem, Brown's men attempted to retake the forts but failed. However, we hear they were able to free more than one hundred of our soldiers held captive there as well as capture over three hundred Redcoats.[56] *Despite the failure of Colonel Brown's raid, it comes as most welcome news. If Brown's men were able to mount an attack so far north of here, it would make sense that the British lines are only sparsely held between here and there, and the enemy's capability to prevent such an attack is nil. That also means few supplies are getting through to the main body of Burgoyne's army here at Stillwater. Gentleman Johnnie will be forced to do something sooner than later. Perhaps he will retreat and try to regain his supply line? Or try to break us here and scamper down to Albany and be rescued by General Clinton? I think we shall soon have him one way or the other.*[57]

September 30, 1777

Here we sit, waiting for Burgoyne to move against us or do something! The worst part of being a soldier is the waiting. Our defense works are completed, and we are just sitting with our pickets out and watching.

At least the British soldiers are busy. They have built two grand redoubts that we can see from our position here on the heights. Morgan's men have been harassing their picket guards beginning in the late afternoon until night hides their targets. I find it fascinating, perhaps gruesomely, to sit and listen to the sound of their rifles and the smack of the bullets when they hit their intended. It's a strange noise, somewhat like the crack of a bullwhip. One can feel utmost sympathy for the poor Redcoat who has earned his last Shilling for King Georgie. They must all be in terror when the first shot is fired. Morgan's men seem to be impervious to their murderous activities and have suffered no losses in their actions, for they know the forest too well to be surprised. Finn is with them in their camp every free moment he can spare from his duties and has become fast friends with more than a few of them. He has been allowed to handle their rifles on occasion, an honor bestowed on few, I'm told.

October 2, 1777

The British continue to build and wait. I'm told they have built cabin shelters and have a bridge across Hudson's River. We are continually reinforced with militia from communities all over New York and New England. Our defenses have become stronger by the day. If Burgoyne's army does indeed decide to settle in for the winter, this army will become weaker, as our militias will return to their homes. Many of the regulars will be mustered out or will desert before spring, and by then the British can bring more troops to New York City and easily crush what's left of us. Now we just play this waiting game.

October 5, 1777

We are told of a move by General Clinton's troops who have apparently left New York City and have moved north against us in an attempt to rescue Burgoyne's army. We have also heard rumors of more attacks by our men against both Fort Ticonderoga and Mount Independence. Other camp stories have General Stark moving to encircle the British in their present location. Gentleman Johnnie has done little during the past three weeks. His men must be getting low on rations, and if his supply line has been endangered by the attacks to the north, they must do something sooner rather than later. [58]

October 6, 1777

Morgan's men have returned this evening from their scout with news of increased activity in the enemy camps. Could this be the move we've been waiting for? Will Burgoyne move on us or cut his losses and retreat to the safety of Ticonderoga? Flip has us making more balls for our muskets, preparing cartridges, and getting our gear in order. He has ordered an extra rum ration for the evening so we may sleep restfully. What tomorrow will bring is unknown. I will give it my best and pray my men and I survive.

That was my last entry for reasons that will become apparent. Although I was a part of this, I must rely on my sometimes-faulty memory and on the tales of others to fully describe my actions in this battle. The Second Battle of Saratoga, sometimes called the battle of Bemis Heights, began the morning of October 7, 1777, when Burgoyne sent a large group of his troops to see how strong our defenses were. We watched as they began to move out of the redoubt nearer the Albany Road and heading towards our position. The orders came for us to move out and engage them; Morgan and Dearborn's men to the right and us on the left. When we moved into position, I could see we faced the Grenadiers of the British army. We held our fire as they maneuvered and began a bayonet charge. When they drew near, we unleashed a volley that dropped most of them in their tracks, including the officer who was leading them. I must confess, I took deliberate aim at him but was never sure if 'twas I who put him down. We followed up with a charge of our own and overtook their artillery, captured some prisoners, and overran their position.

In the meantime, Morgan and Dearborn ran into the British light infantry and did the same to them. There was, however, a column of Germans in between our two forces, and they were now in danger of being enveloped by us and Morgan's force. More of our troops came into the battle. A general officer who was rallying the Germans, and any British soldiers he could find, suddenly went down just as his men were beginning to hold fast and our men were beginning to waver. I have been told he was a picked mark by one of Morgan's men. Taking him out of the battle at that moment was most opportune. Almost simultaneously, Arnold appeared, calling to us, urging us on, leading a charge on his horse. A moment of exhilaration gripped every American on the field, and we couldn't help but follow. We poured into the Germans with a fury and broke into hand-to-hand combat.

I can remember a few details here and there and distinctly can still feel the sharp pain in my shoulder from a musket ball. I also can still see the Hessian's bayonet as he lunged for my belly. I blocked his thrust away but not enough for him to miss me completely. He shoved that skewer right though my left thigh, and I screamed in agony. Then he went down with a scream of his own, holding his head where Flip's musket had left its mark. Etched in my memory, I still can see Flip's expression; indeed, it is one I'll never be able to forget. It was a look of surprise, disbelief, and bewilderment, and then I could see the bayonet as it made its way through his chest. He died almost instantly and fell across my legs. Finn or Quentin, I couldn't tell which one, dispatched the German who had killed Flip and then headed into the redoubt with the rest of our men.

I began to swoon and can only remember bits and pieces from here on. I came to once to see my German assailant on his knees, ripping the white lining out of his uniform and staunching the blood in both my shoulder and thigh wounds. I watched then as he grabbed his head, which he had also wrapped with cloth, and toppled over next to me. Hours may have passed. I can't recollect how long I laid there. The German kept moving to and from sleep, moaning from time to time. At one point, I remember sharing some water with him from my canteen.

PART VIII

AFTERMATH

It was near nightfall when Finn and Quentin came to remove me from the field where I had fallen. Finn was ready to put the German out of his misery when I became coherent enough to stop him, explaining what he had done for my wounds. Quentin spoke to him in Dutch, being the former slave of a Dutch family, though it was something I remember as surprising at the time. We had never heard him do this before. The German told him his name was Werner Dussel and he was from Brunswig. Quentin made him understand we weren't going to hurt him. He asked if he could stay with us, as he was ready to desert anyway and never go back to Germany again. After lying Flip's body to rest on the field near where he died, we took Werner back to our camp hospital. Finn and Quentin were able to make the surgeons believe he was a New York militia man who had gotten mixed into our unit and, being a Dutchman, spoke little English.

When we settled into the unit hospital, Quentin instructed Werner to say he was Werner Van Impe, a New York Dutchman farmer and Quentin's owner. It was a masquerade that we played out until our convalescence was over. As the Fates would have it, Werner and I would remain together for some time.

While I was in hospital, Burgoyne's army was surrounded, cut off from retreat and his supplies. General Clinton's men returned to New York City. All in all, 'twas a magnificent feat of arms and a great victory for us Americans. General Arnold had been wounded again in the same thigh as Quebec and was in the same hospital as us for a time, fighting this time to keep his leg. General Gates received all the glory and accolades from Congress due our Connecticut general. Arnold's pride was mightily injured at Saratoga's end; he could endure the leg, but the proud man never recovered from his other wound.

Shortly after the surrender, Werner and I were sent back to Portsmouth, New Hampshire, to finish our recovery. Once again, Pierse Long became my benefactor, making sure I was comfortable and providing me with a place to live. When I and Werner were fully recovered, he arranged for us to work in one of his warehouses along the docks.

By then, Finn and Quentin had headed south with Morgan's men, Finn joining their unit and Quentin tagging along. I still had a desire to be with my mother and sisters but didn't want to leave Portsmouth just yet, as winter was setting in quickly. Finn and Quentin had tried to contact them, but to no avail. A letter from Finn arrived, saying he was moving even further south with Morgan's. I was beginning to get restless and vowed that by spring I would go to the Jerseys and find my family. Or at least try.

Werner and I worked throughout the winter of 1777 and 1778. I often thought Pierse Long knew Werner wasn't a Dutch farmer, but he never let on that he did. We were well paid and fed, comfortable in our quarters. I told Werner my plans, and he wanted to come along and help. I tried to talk him out of it; as a deserter from the enemy, he would have been executed for his deed, but he wouldn't hear of it. He had become Werner Van Impe, Dutch farmer from New York.

It was a rainy April day when one of Long's ships came in bearing cargo I least expected, Quentin, my mother, and my sisters. Also with Quentin was his new bride, Magdalene, a free woman of color from

Jersey. They had met shortly after Quentin's arrival, and she knew of my family's whereabouts, and she took him to meet them. Quentin had contacted Long and made arrangements to come to Portsmouth.

Then Quentin made the rest of his plans clear. He told us of the nearby Vermont Republic, which, he said, had outlawed slavery. He and Magdalene could live there free, like White people, own their very own farm or business, and never have to be beholden to anyone ever again. He had already bought a piece of land in the new village of South Woodstock and said there was plenty more where that came from. I had saved quite a tidy sum working for Pierse Long and was ready for the change. I was never cut out for warehousing, anyway.

As for Werner, he had taken a quick shine to my sister Rachel and wasn't going to let her slip away from him. We said our goodbyes to Pierse Long; I could never be able to repay his kindness and support. But he understood and sent us on our way with his best wishes and one of his wagons.

So there it is. I married Jemma Greer in 1781, daughter of another farmer who had recently settled in the area. We have four children; Isaac Junior, Sarah, Sally, and Pierse. Werner married Rachel, and they moved again to Portsmouth where Werner went back to work for Mr. Long. They have four children as well.

My sister Peggy married James Dunn, and it was one of her sons' wives who put me up to all of this. Quentin and Magdalene settled just a piece down the road. When Vermont joined the States in 1791, Quentin maintained his free status and now has an equal voice in running the town, along with me and my brother-in-law, James. No man will dare speak against him when I'm around.

My shoulder wound has healed and never gives me a wince of pain, despite the weather, but that skewer wound Werner laid on my thigh still comes back to haunt me every cold, damp winter's eve.

After all these years, I'm still perplexed about General Arnold's turning coat. Make no mistake, and every veteran of Saratoga as well will tell you, too, how he won that battle for us and indeed procured our independence by doing so. Why he ever left us, I'll never understand.

And Finn, what became of him I don't know. He never did find out what happened to his family. We suspect they were murdered by that Cowboy faction of Tories. He last visited here sometime around 1818 or so, telling grand stories of how he helped whip Tarleton and Cornwallis and single-handedly won our war of Independence. Claimed he served in the 1812 war, fought against Tecumseh at Tippecanoe and with Andy Jackson at New Orleans. Said he was heading west, out to a new territory called Missouri. 'Course, that's before it became a state. Never heard anything more from him since.

I was barely 20 years old when we moved here. It's 1828, and I'm seventy now. Most of my family is still around these parts. Pierse served in the 1812 war and fought in the battle of Plattsburg. There hasn't been any fighting to speak of since, and peace has come to our land. Slavery is still an issue but doesn't exist here in Vermont.

We've made a prosperous sheep farm and have a prize flock of Merinos whose wool fetches some mighty high prices. My brother-in-law James and I run the place, but our sons pitch in greatly. Quentin and his lot share pasture, shearing, and shipping, and we've come to live a comfortable life as can be. However, the memories of our days as soldiers still linger. It still staggers me how we managed to pull it off.

I can only hope our efforts will not ever be in vain, as we have created a nation unlike any other on Earth. Two years ago, this nation celebrated its fiftieth birthday. I can still remember hearing the Declaration being read by Colonel St. Clair. The words still ring true. We've survived as a nation. We bow to no king, emperor, czar, or pope, and only the blight of slavery keeps us from living up to the ideals we set forth in the Declaration. But that abomination will pass from our shores, too, and we will become a beacon of freedom for all the world to copy. Of that I'm sure. So, dear reader, I put down my pen and render my pages shut, leaving my memories for my family and ancestors. May we live up to our principles and be worthy, as a nation, of the sacrifices Flip and all the others made for us.

AFTERWORD

Isaac Kendall died in 1836 at the age of 76. He was survived by his sons and daughters, whose kin still live around the area.

Werner Van Impe (Dussel) lived near Portsmouth, New Hampshire until 1845, when he died a fairly wealthy shipping merchant, leaving his legacy to his sons and grandchildren. He was 82.

Quentin Freeman died in 1840, though he was unsure of how old he ever was, having no record of his birth. One of his grandsons served the Union in the 121st Regiment of Colored Troops during the Civil War.

Benjamin "Finn" McCool, as it would seem, served out the Revolution and fought in the War of 1812. He went west, according to Kendall, sometime after 1818 and never returned to the East. He has no known date of death or whereabouts at this time. At least, that's conjecture.

AUTHOR'S NOTE

First of all, I must tell the reader two things. First, there was no Isaac Kendall, Flip Johnson, Finn McCool, or Quentin Freeman. Second, there were hundreds, even thousands, of men like them. The events covered in this work are also real, as are some of the characters, such as Arnold, Kosciusko, and Gates. Kendall and the others are a product of research, firsthand knowledge of historic sites like Mount Independence, and my imagination. Men from all walks of life served, suffered, existed, lived, and died there. What I have done here is to construct a character that would show what it was like to be a soldier stationed at Mount Independence and what life would have been like for that soldier. I tried to put in as many items of interest that I have garnered from years of working at Mount Independence, where I have had access to papers, letters, official documents, and such. By putting many of the events from those papers into life-like situations using these characters, I hope I have given the reader an idea of what the real soldiers of the American Revolution went through and experienced.

ENDNOTES

1   Author's note: Charles Burrall's (sometimes spelled Burrell's) regiment mustered in the beginning of January 1776 and was sent to the Northern Army. They were in Lake George by April, then were sent to Cedars, 43 miles above Montreal, along with Bedell's New Hampshire Regiment and 2 pieces of artillery. Relieved of their duties at Cedars, they next went to Deschambault, Quebec. While at Deschambault, they became engulfed in the retreat and infected with the smallpox outbreak that nearly destroyed the Northern Army. They fought in the battle of Three Rivers (Trois Riviers) on May 5, 1776 and were in Chambley by late May, awaiting evacuation with the rest of the army. It is most likely that Isaac Kendall and his replacement group did not catch up with the regiment before they headed up the lake to Crown Point and Ticonderoga.

2   The Crown Point Military Road stretches from the site of Fort Number Four in New Hampshire through the state of Vermont over the Green Mountains and the Taconics to Crown Point, New York. A branch of this road, known as the Ticonderoga branch, connects with Mt. Independence and Fort Ticonderoga.

3   The Crown Point Military Road was built in 1758 and 1759 by General Amherst to connect the Connecticut River supply lines with the then frontier outposts of Crown Point and Ticonderoga. It had fallen into much disuse by 1775, but the capture of Fort Ticonderoga by the Colonial forces in May of 1775 brought the road back into prominence and was used to shift men and materials to the forts along Lake Champlain and Montreal. An improved branch was constructed to connect Fort Ticonderoga with the main road, which also connected Mt. Independence

and its installations. The corduroy Kendall is referring to are logs that are laid into the muddy areas to keep men and wagons from sinking.

4   This tavern was probably Gaylord's Tavern near present day Eureka and Springfield, Vermont. Some controversy exists as to whether or not Gaylord's was there in 1776. The 1895 *History of the Town of Springfield, Vermont* by Hubbard & Dartt quotes, "There was a tavern at Eureka very early called the Gaylord Tavern," and also states, "…. Many farmers kept public houses and there was no lack of taverns."

5   Almost certainly, Isaac was at what is now Ludlow, Vermont. The water he is referring to is most likely the Black River. Ludlow lies in a valley between the Green Mountains and would have been an oasis in the spring of 1776.

6   Kendall is probably at the high point of the Green Mountains at the area known today as "Summit." It would have been miles from the nearest settlement in 1776 and very desolate.

7   Hampshire Grants

8   Kendall's fear was not uncommon; a smallpox epidemic revenged the colonies from 1775-1782, striking all indiscriminately. Many colonies banned inoculations; Washington considered inoculating the entire army at Cambridge, Massachusetts, in March of 1776, but opted for quarantining soldiers as soon as they got the disease. In February 1776, Benedict Arnold ordered that, "The Surgeons of the Army are forbid, under the severest penalty, to inoculate any person," with cashiering and court martial as a risk if they did. This move by Arnold would prove to be disastrous, as the Northern Army was ravaged with the disease by spring. Still, men did get the vaccine, sometimes even giving it to themselves with pins under fingernails. Trent probably saw the effects of the disease when he was in Canada and took it upon himself to get these men the vaccine. By 1777, George Washington decided on inoculation for the entire army who had not had the disease. For much more information of the disease, read *Pox Americana: The Great Smallpox Epidemic of 1775-82*, by Elizabeth Anne Fenn. The name of the doctor Trent found in the Rutland area has no record.

9   This is the site of Fort Ranger, which was completed by 1778 for use by Vermont units. Present day Carris Reels occupies this site.

10   This is the site of Sunderland Falls in present day Proctor, Vermont, previously known as the Great Falls. The rocky outcrops Kendall talks about are marble since they are moving through part of the Marble Valley.

11   The Ticonderoga Branch splits from the main road in present day

Sudbury, Vermont.

12   Brigadier General John Thomas was a well-liked commander who refused to be vaccinated nor did he allow any of his men to be. He got the disease on May 21 and died from it on June 2, 1776. He was replaced by Brigadier General John Sullivan. The battle of Three Rivers, Trois Rivieres, was fought on June 8, 1776 in Quebec. It was a disaster for the Colonials, who were outnumbered by fresh British troops. Carlton, the British commander, let the Americans escape because he felt the tale they'd spread would do more good than capturing them. Casualties were around 400 American dead and 200-plus captured for a British loss of less than a dozen.

13   On June 24, a raiding party of Native Americans surprised a group of men from the 6th Pennsylvania, who were fishing away from camp. They killed four and took six prisoners before escaping, despite an alarm being given. Two days later, the army shifted south to Isle La Motte and then to Crown Point, where they arrived on July 2, 1776.

14   This position was referred to by General Wayne as, "…to be the last part of the world that God made and I have some ground to believe it was finished in the dark…"

15   A "Flip" was a concoction of about two-thirds a mug of beer or ale, with a large "shot" of rum added. It was then sweetened with sugar or molasses (or something sweet) and stirred with a red-hot poker, which caused it to boil and steam. It was a very popular drink, especially during the winter months.

16   The Declaration of Independence was read to the troops on July 27, 1776. The name was changed to Mt. Independence in honor of the Declaration.

17   Franklin, Samuel Chase, and Charles Carroll, along with Father John Carroll, a French-speaking Catholic priest, left for Montreal in March of 1776. Their mission was to convince the People of Quebec to join the American cause. A French printer and a printing press were also brought along. The group did not arrive in Montreal until late April, about the time of the American retreat from Quebec City. Franklin left Montreal after a two-week stay, accompanied by Father Carroll. The others stayed until the last of the American Army left for points south. It is possible that Flip saw Dr. Franklin and Father Carroll on their way to Albany when they passed through the Fort Ticonderoga area. Upon reaching Albany, General Phillip Schuyler provided a coach that took Franklin and Carroll back to Philadelphia, where they arrived in early June.

18   Kendall is referring to the Jersey Redoubt on the Ticonderoga

side of the lake.

19   Benjamin Hazen's men were part of the Fort Chambly garrison during the American retreat from Canada in May and June of 1776. Hazen and Arnold clashed over goods confiscated from Montreal merchants that Arnold wanted sent to Chambly for shipment south. Hazen refused to sign for them, declaring they were property of friends in Montreal. Most of the goods were plundered and lost during the retreat, and Arnold wanted to court martial Hazen, but the British arrived too quickly to do so. Upon arrival at Ticonderoga, Hazen was given a court martial and acquitted. Finding the judge to be biased led Arnold to reopen the procedure in December of 1776 with the result being the same: acquittal. Hazen then charged Arnold with stealing from the Montreal merchant. Arnold was cleared of these charges in another hearing in 1777.

20   Arnold built a total of twelve boats during the summer of 1776. He had four others, which made up the squadron total of sixteen. These would be available to meet the enemy fleet whenever the British began to move or could be used to attack their installations on the northern end of the lake.

21   Colonel Jeduthan Baldwin was the chief engineer of the defenses and was instrumental in designing and constructing the extensive defenses at both Ticonderoga and Mount Independence. The Horseshoe Battery became the dominant artillery position of Mount Independence and could prevent any ships from reaching the shores of the installations. The rumor about General Howe was just as Kendall mentioned it at the time. Howe had, however, landed his large force on Long Island and was beginning his campaign against Washington for control of New York.

22   Benjamin Whitcomb, leader of Whitcomb's Rangers, did indeed ambush and mortally wound British general Gordon on or about August 12, 1776, prompting Governor General Sir Guy Carleton to issue the warning Kendall quotes in his writing.

23   Captain Jacobus Wynkoop, believing himself to be the admiral of Lake Champlain, continually argued with Arnold, often countermanding his orders until Arnold could take no more and had Wynkoop arrested for court martial. Rather than putting Wynkoop on trial, Arnold allowed Wynkoop to go home.

24   Benedict Arnold was given command by the Continental Congress to take Fort Ticonderoga, but when he and his few men arrived in the Hampshire Grants, they met up with Ethan Allen and his Green Mountain Boys. Allen's men refused Arnold's command and followed Allen's lead, capturing the fort, and Crown Point as well. In May of 1775,

Arnold was alongside, only nominally sharing command.

25   Lt. Col. William Bonds of Gardner's 2nd Massachusetts Regiment died of yellow fever on August 31, 1776.

26   Kendall is referring to poultices of hot, moist substances that were covered with flannel. These were thought to ease pain and swelling. Anodynes were made of laudanum (an opium derivative), a carrier such as saffron or anise, and a little wine.

27   Kendall is referring to quinoa bark, which had been discovered to relieve malaria symptoms.

28   This report was erroneous.

29   Day claims he was captured and forced to serve. His testimony alerted Arnold and the others to the strength of the British fleet and forces.

30   The term Hessian is a misnomer, as there were troops hired from seven different German principalities (Hesse Hanau, Hesse Cassel, Brunswick, Anhalt Zerbst, Anspach, Baeruth, and Waldeck) to serve in North America. They were demonized by American propaganda and greatly feared by the troops that met them. A scheme known as the "Tobacco Papers" was devised by Ben Franklin, which offered land and citizenship if they deserted. These were printed on tobacco paper and distributed throughout Canada.

31   Although Kendall wasn't at the battle of Valcour, Arnold's exploits there became well-known to all the men, mostly due to his popularity among them. Kendall's version is concise and accurate.

32   Carleton's attack on the Fort Ticonderoga complex is just as Kendall tells it. Carlton's decision not to continue his attack was due to a few factors. First of all, the strength of the American's position and number of troops available to repulse his efforts became more obvious to Carleton as he drew closer. Secondly, it was getting later into October, and there was already snow capping both the Adirondacks and the Green Mountains. Lake Champlain was already beginning to freeze in places, and winter quarters began to look like a better idea. Within a week, the British withdrew to Montreal.

33   "Cowboys" was a term used for Loyalist marauders who had taken the role of irregulars trying to terrorize those who opposed King George III's rule. They were active in many areas but especially around Tory-leaning New York City and western Connecticut.

34   Pierse Long's New Hampshire Regiment was formed in May of 1776 in and around Portsmouth, probably to protect Long's shipping business.

35   Franklin left Philadelphia aboard the sloop *Reprisal* and arrived in France on December 3, 1776.

36   Colonel Jeduthan Baldwin was the main engineer at Mount Independence. He laid out most of the Mount during the spring of 1777. He undertook all the projects Kendall mentions with little or no other help from the high command. He charged himself with all the details of construction and supervision and completed every task, although the hospital was not completed when the British captured Mount Independence in July of 1777. The general Hospital's plans were laid out in March 1777, and woodcutting began sometime around mid-month. The actual construction, according to Baldwin's Journal, didn't begin until May. Baldwin also mentions dining with some doctors in the hospital on June 6 and again on June 20. General Phillip Schuyler's letter to Congress, dated June 25, mentions the unfinished rooms of the hospital and voices his concerns as to when it will actually house sick soldiers. Considering that the position was abandoned just slightly more than a week later, the question can be raised as to whether or not this particular hospital was ever used by the American troops. However, James Thatcher, a surgeon's mate, mentions orders given to evacuate the sick and wounded along with the hospital's stores the night of July 6. It is almost certain the British used the facility for their casualties and sick.

37   The Great Bridge was a masterpiece of engineering, which still fascinates and astounds modern day visitors to Mt. Independence. It was constructed as Kendall relates but remains a mystery as to exactly how the piers were lowered into the lake so precisely.

38   St Clair's 12-year-old son, Daniel, did accompany him and was sent back as soon as his father could assess the situation. He arranged all the troops into four brigades:

1st: Commanding; Roche Fermoy
Hale's New Hampshire
Bradford's Massachusetts
Marshall's Massachusetts

2nd: Commanding; John Patterson
Cilley's 1st New Hampshire
Scammell's 3rd New Hampshire
Jackson's Massachusetts

3rd: Commanding; Enoch Poor
Francis' Massachusetts
Brewer's Massachusetts
Warner's Additional

4th: Mt. Independence; Pierse Long
Long's New Hampshire
Well's Massachusetts
Leonard's Massachusetts
Ebenezer Steven's Artillery Battalion
For a total of around 3,500 effectives.

39   On June 20, St. Clair held an officer's council and the decision was made to abandon the works at Ticonderoga and defend Mt. Independence. Plans were also drawn up for a retreat from both positions. It was on this day that Burgoyne began moving his men out of St. Johns.

40   July 2nd, Simon Fraser's advance corps reached the defenses at Mt. Hope, drove off the guards stationed there to the French Lines, and began a firefight where some 3,000 rounds and 8 artillery shots were exchanged. It was a complete waste of gunpowder by both sides, resulting in one British soldier killed and two wounded.

41   General Roche Fermoy set his quarters and papers on fire sometime around 3:00 am, turning the retreat into a desperate race to escape since the British now knew the installation was being evacuated. Whether the fire was purposely or accidently set is moot.

42   Kendall's description of Long's Regiment's retreat from the Ticonderoga / Mt. Independence complex is incredibly accurate. He captures the confident, leisurely attitude of the men, along with the foraging of the medicinal wine supply. Captain Gray's company of Scammell's Regiment was at Skenesboro, and Colonel Van Renssalaer's militia of 400 strong joined Long's Regiment at Fort Ann after their retreat from Lake George's Fort George. Confusion and surprise played a major role in the British attack on Long, in which nearly all the material removed from Mt. Independence was captured or destroyed, along with the last five of Arnold's navy.

43   Once again, Kendall's description is well-detailed. He had no way of knowing that it was a lone British officer who had given the war-whoop and deceived Long's men into thinking reinforcements had come. In this skirmish, Colonel Van Renssalear was wounded in the hip and crippled for life.

44   Burgoyne's vast supply lines stretched not only northward to Montreal but also eastward to Quebec City and the United Kingdom. Totaling some 900 wagons, this ponderous column moved slowly through the path that stretched between Fort Ann and Fort Edward. So effective was the American plan that it took nearly three weeks to move the twelve miles. Along with the hot, humid weather and biting insects, it's no wonder

the journey took so long.

45   Kendall, Finn, and Quentin witnessed one of the most controversial events of Burgoyne's campaign: the murder of Jane McCrae. There are many variations of this murder, and this one seems to be the most plausible. Positive proof of the cause of death using forensic archeology was attempted, but when the body was exhumed, it was found to be missing its skull. According to archeologist David R. Starbuck who exhumed the McCrae grave site in 2005, "and discovered the remains of a 20"x 24"box containing the skeletons of two women—but only one skull, from a very old woman who had definitely not been scalped."(quote from archives of Plymouth State University, The Mystery of the Second Body). Starbuck's DNA testing proved the skull was that of Sara McNeil, who was the older women with Jane when she was murdered. McNeil was the cousin of British General Simon Fraser and probably too valuable to kill. Fraser was killed at Second Saratoga, the Battle of Bemis Heights, by Morgan's rifleman Timothy Murphy. The McCrae story has been made into legend, and the true version of her death remains difficult to substantiate. The real substance of the murder lies in the reaction to McCrae's death from both the local inhabitants and how it affected Burgoyne's campaign.

46   William Howe was to meet Burgoyne in Albany, New York, along with Barry St. Leger's force coming from the Niagara frontier, thus splitting up the colony of New York and separating New England from the rest of the nation. This would isolate New England, and then the colonies could be subdued in smaller groups.

47   The battle of Oriskany occurred August 6, 1777 in the Mohawk Valley of New York, in present day Oneida County. It was the first battle of Barry St. Leger's move on Albany from the Niagara frontier. Few battles demonstrate the civil war nature of the American Revolution than this one, as it pitted neighbor against neighbor, ideology against ideology.

48   The American Revolution effectively ended the Iroquois Confederation. The Oneida and Tuscarora supported the Americans, and the Mohawks, Onondaga, Cayuga, and Seneca fought for the British. At Oriskany, for the first time in three centuries, members of the Six Nations fought against each other.

49   Burgoyne indeed did try to punish the Native American who murdered Jane McCrae, but in doing so, he alienated his Native American allies who returned to their homes in large numbers. Burgoyne's advisor for the Native Americans was Chevalier La Luc de la Corne, a Canadian of French descent, who warned Burgoyne that he would alienate the braves if he took action against them. Just the idea of being punished for such a small offense was enough to send them home, despite La Luc's promises

of more rum and plunder. By the beginning of August, most of the Native Americans were gone. Those who remained were primarily Mohawks and other members of the Iroquois Confederation and Christian "civilized" Native Americans.

50   The Republic of Vermont was created on July 8, 1777, when a constitution was adopted at Windsor. A vote to free the area from the rest of the colonies had taken place the previous winter, but the Continental Congress refused entry into the new United States, mostly due to New York's blockage of Vermont's request. Not to be put off by Congress, Vermont's town representatives met at Windsor just as Mt. Independence was being captured and the battle of Hubbardton was being fought. A thunderstorm prevented the delegates from fleeing in terror. They made the best of their time by adopting a constitution, complete with a bill of rights and a clause outlawing slavery, making the new republic the first place in what is now the United States to do so. Unsure of what the populace would do, but aware of their new independence from everyone else, Burgoyne referred to the new republic, saying that it "abounds in the most active and most rebellious race of the continent and hangs like a gathering storm on my left."

51   The battle of Bennington occurred on August 16, 1777, when Burgoyne dispatched a force of over 500 to seize stores of supplies and horses at the nearby town of Bennington (the supplies didn't exist). The British (mostly German) force was attacked by General John Stark, who rallied much of the local militias and the Green Mountain Boys. A relief column arriving on the scene was also defeated by Stark. Burgoyne's force of just over 1,000 men was completely routed, and only around 100 made it back to the British lines. Kendall's figures of over 1,500 are a little higher than the actual number the British lost at Bennington.

52   Fort Stanwix was the "key" to the Mohawk Valley and needed to be taken if St. Leger's move on Albany was to be successful. St. Leger arrived at the fort and laid siege to it, beginning on August 2, 1777. A large portion of this siege force was drawn for the battle of Oriskany, greatly weakening the force before Stanwix. In the midst of a political battle over Stanwix and Burgoyne's movement south, General Phillip Schuyler dispatched Benedict Arnold to lift the siege. Arnold used Han Yost, a mentally challenged individual who the Native Americans considered sacred, to inform them that Arnold was coming with a force "numerous as the leaves on the trees." They took him at his word, looted the British camp, and went home. With the loss of his Native Americans and the heavy losses of Loyalists at Oriskany, St. Leger gathered what forces he had left and retreated to Niagara, thus ending his campaign for Albany.

53   Kendall's writings cover the first battle of Saratoga, and his 2nd New Hampshire's role agree with most contemporary and modern accounts of the battle. There are many well-written works that cover Saratoga that may be of interest to the reader.

54   News from Clinton reached Burgoyne that he was moving north up the Hudson to Burgoyne's relief.

55   Arnold was relieved of command after protesting Gate's letter to the Continental Congress, in which Gates did not credit Arnold for his role in the First Battle of Saratoga. Arnold took exception, an argument ensued, and Gates removed Arnold from command but allowed him to remain with the army under tent arrest.

56   On September 18, Colonel John Brown's 500 Americans failed in an attack on the British garrisons at Fort Ticonderoga and Mount Independence. While he assaulted Ti, Colonel Samuel Johnson hit the defenses of Mt. Independence. Although neither attack was successful, the attack shook British morale and threatened their supply lines. It did little damage otherwise, although Brown did free 118 American prisoners and captured 330 enemy soldiers.

57   Clinton moved troops north from New York City. Although he took some strategic installations south of Albany, notably Forts Clinton and Montgomery, his half-hearted effort never made it that far. He received 1,700 additional troops in late September and tried to move the American garrison from their posts by moving some frigates up the Hudson. Messages sent from Clinton to Burgoyne were all intercepted, and he was unable to come to Burgoyne's rescue.

58   New Hampshire's John Stark and a new force of militia moved between Burgoyne's position and Fort Edward, helping to surround Burgoyne, cut his supply lines and was a major part in convincing Burgoyne to surrender.

www.ingramcontent.com/pod-product-compliance
Lightning Source LLC
Chambersburg PA
CBHW031056310726
48969CB00007B/2303